# Amalia

**Omar G. Glove**

# Contents

# 0.

She looks innocent, but she's not.

Amalia Ferrari, a name many feared and many envied. A name that would give men and women nightmares. A name every woman wishes to have and every women envy. A woman every man wishes to have and touch.

Saying that Amalia has no enemies, would be a lie. In fact, every single person she works with or not, is her enemy. Everyone outside her house, is her enemy.

Why?

A question she always asks herself, but finally found the answer.

Fear.

Yes, fear is the answer. People fear her, they fear her power and wealth. They fear her genius and manipulating mind.

On the other hand, saying that Amalia is a good person would be another lie. She's not.

In general, she's a bitch who's greedy for power. She would do anything to stay at the top, anything.

It's not that she doesn't have good in her, she does, but the good inside her only comes out whenever she allows it to. Only when she's in the mood.

Even though, she has a very strong, manipulating personality, no one hates her. They can't. In fact, they admire her. Her enemies admire her. They want to be like her, but in order to do that, they have to cross her, meaning, taking her out of the equation.

To stay safe, she needed one bodyguard. Only one. One who she can trust and depend on.

It's so hard for Amalia to trust. Actually, she only trusts two in her life and they are Annie and Gus.

Annie is her nanny, whom she had since she was a little girl. Annie never left her side, even after the death of her parents. She took good care of her and was like a mother to her, and Amalia would forever be grateful.

Gus however, was her dog. Her 5 year old German shepherd dog, who loves her more than anything. She loves him too tho. A lot.

Trusting a third person is very hard for her, but she had to since she's in danger. She had to open her heart and trust another.

# 1. Amalia Ferrari

AMALIA

Blood.

I hate it a lot. I hate the sight of it, especially when I see it every month for 5 days.

Periods are hard, but I am so thankful that I get mine.

Trying to stand up and ignore my cramps, I slowly step forward into my balcony. The view my room has is beyond astonishing. I have always been one who loves nature, it keeps my mind at peace and I always feel relaxed.

I glance at the birds flying in the sky and close my eyes, taking deep breaths. I just love mornings. I love the sound of birds chirping in the mornings. They wake me up every day at 7a.m, and I don't even have to put my alarm on.

I walk back to my room and get ready for the day. Yesterday, one of my partners, told me what the circle has been planning. The circle is a group of elites; me included, who meet every week to discuss business and future plans. I did not go last week, and they took this opportunity to talk about me. Luckily, my closest partner: Jeremy Stone, told me what they're planning, and that's to end me. They want me out of the circle and so they voted. Most of the votes voted a no and so they won, and those little who voted for a yes, will probably go for a riskier solution.

This solution I know very well. I am not stupid, and I do not work with people I do not know how they think. That's why I know they will hire a hitman to kill me, but unfortunately, it's not going to be that easy to get rid of me.

I'm Amalia Ferrari and I am not easy to kill.

Entering my walk-in closet, I pick up some dresses to wear for today. I place them three on the table and take a good look at each one of them.

The problem with me is that I have to look perfect. It's not that I am obsessed with what people think of me or if they like how I look, it's that I am obsessed with how I think and see myself.

I have to look pretty to feel good.

Deciding on wearing the tight, red, mid-thigh dress, I undressed and put it on.

I then walked to my shoe rack and picked out a pair of white heels.

I never wore casual clothes at home. I always dress up as if I am going out. Only when the house is fully empty that I be myself and that's mostly after 9p.m when everyone leaves.

Yes, I am not myself around people. I act like a completely different person. A person who is mean and manipulative, not that I am not truly that, but I am meaner and more manipulative around people. I love to play games and I always win them.

I truly believe that each one of us has a different side when they're alone. A different person within.

Walking downstairs, I see Annie standing at the end of the stairs, holding a tray with tea in it, waiting for me to come down. Annie is my mother. Not my biological mother, but still. She's the one who stood by me and never betrayed me. Her love and kindness are what helped me become the woman I am today.

It's really funny that most of the times some people say or more specifically, some men say that women are weak, or they are not smart enough to become something big. But I am here to prove them wrong. We are not weak, and we are not stupid. In fact, we are smart and strong, and we can do whatever we want in this shitty world.

Take me as an example, all the men I've met fear me. They wish to be me and own what I have.

I worked so hard to have what I have right now. I didn't inherit many things from my parents other than a farmhouse they left for me. I built myself step by step and I made myself by myself—with the help of Annie of course.

Every person reaches their goal with the help of either or both parents. They don't have to help financially or anything, it's just the kindness and the love they show that makes you stronger. Of course, some people reach their goals without the help of their parents, even some with the help of their friends. For me, it's Annie and Gus; my dog.

Right now, I am in a place where I am greedy for power. A lot of people hate me for that, but honestly, I don't give a shit. Hate me all you want, but at the end, I am going to win.

"Buongiorno Ms." Annie greets with a bright smile that makes up your entire day.

(Good morning)

"Buongiorno mamma—how many times do I have to tell you to call me by my name?" I greet back and scold her.

(Good morning mom)

I can't have my mother call me Ms.

"You know I say that out of habit—besides, everyone who works here has to learn how to call you." She explains.

Walking into the living room with her following, I ask, "where is Antonia?"

Antonia is my secretary. I don't really like her; I might fire her today.

"She hasn't come, yet." Annie nervously replies, knowing that I will fire Antonia as soon as she says that.

As if on cue, Antonia walks in.

"Ms. Ferrari, please forgive me, there was too much traffic!" She exclaims.

I turn her way and scowl. I hate laziness, a lot. The fact that her work starts at 9a.m is even a mercy. Most people start at 7, which only means that there isn't a lot of traffic since most people already went to work.

"You are fired Antonia." I smile happily. I really hate her. The way she looks at and talks to me is just so annoying.

"Ms. Amalia, please!" She cried.

"You don't call me by my first name! Now get out of my face." I yell in my authoritative voice.

She turns around and strolls out.

"Weren't you a little bit harsh?" Annie asks softly.

Annie is the only one who can question me and yell at me. Not that she had ever yelled, but I wouldn't mind. In fact, she and Gus are the only ones I care about. I am only kind to them...and maybe kids and babies.

"No, I wasn't. To me, this was kindness." I yawned and sat on my expensive couch.

"I need a new secretary and a personal bodyguard." I order Annie.

"A bodyguard? For what?" She curiously asks.

"I might be a target, so I need a trustworthy bodyguard." I explain earning a gasp. I just roll my eyes.

"Oh god! You have to stay at home till we find one."

As much as I love Annie, sometimes she's so dramatic.

"I can take care of myself Annie, but not all the time, that's why I need a bodyguard." I explain and drink up my tea Annie got me.

"Okay, Amalia. I will find both." She nods and leaves, but not before thanking her.

I walk around the mansion checking on every employee and their work. As soon as each one of them sees me, fear becomes evident on their faces. I don't know why, maybe because I can fire them and they need the job, but other than that, I do not look scary.

Well, maybe...I do.

"Ms. Ferrari." The chef; Ezekiel, says and bows his head.

"What's for breakfast today?" I ask looking around the kitchen.

"Omelets with French bread and pancakes." He replies excitedly. He loves food so much and I admire him for that. In fact, I hired him because of his passion towards food.

"Good, I like." I nod and walk out of the kitchen.

I make my way towards the laundry room and open the door, entering. This room is huge due to the fact that we have a lot of laundry to do. The house is big and as a part of their jobs, they can clean their clothes here.

"Ms. Ferrari." Ashelia greets.

Believe it or not, but I do know every employee's name. I don't hire people and forget their names; I am not that mean.

"Ashelia." I nod back. She seems off and scared.

Suddenly, I hear a voice. A kid's voice.

I walk towards the sound to find a boy sitting under the table, hiding.

"Whose kid is this?" I softly ask, don't want to scare him.

"I-It's mine." Ashelia replies nervously.

"What is he doing here?" I ask, looking at her.

"I am so sorry Ms. Ferrari; I didn't know where else to take him. His babysitter quit and I couldn't find another." She pleads.

I look at the kid and my expression soften. I could show compassion only once, right?

"It's fine, Ashelia. Next time, do inform me, don't be scared." I say.

"Now kid, how about we play outside?" I ask in a robotic tone.

Everyone in the laundry room gasps and a look of surprise covered their faces.

"You really don't have to..." Ashelia hesitantly says. I send her a glare and she shuts up.

The boy nods with a smile and walks after me.

We walk towards the garden and as soon as we walk out, Gus runs towards the boy and licks him.

That's a first.

The boy giggles and soon they sit on the grass and play together. I sit on one of the chairs and read todays newspaper.

Juliet Loke has been arrested for embezzlement. She has been sent to prison for 25 years for stealing almost 500 million dollars. The police also suspect another two, but no evidence has been found yet.

Wow Juliet, you got caught that fast? Stupid.

I mean, if people are going to commit theft, the least they could do is do it right. Don't get caught, it's embarrassing for god's sake.

I close the newspaper and glance at the kid. He is still playing with Gus and to my surprise, Gus likes him a lot.

Few minutes pass when the boy walks towards me.

"What's your name?" He asks curiously.

"Amalia." I give the smallest smile. A genuine one.

"My mother says you are scary." He says making me arch my brow and smirk.

"Of course, she will—what's your name?"

"It's Angelo." He replies shyly.

"Well Angelo, do you think I am scary?" I ask and he shook his head right and left as a no.

"Good."

We walk back inside, and he goes to his mother, while I go to the dining room to eat my breakfast. Annie comes in after a minute or so.

"So, you found any?" I ask after swallowing the food.

"Yes, I found both actually—regarding your secretary, I found two, so you can interview them, and for bodyguards, I found 3. They are coming tomorrow for the interview at 3p.m."

"Good. Grazie." I say.

(Thank you)

Finishing our breakfast, I walk to the gym to exercise.

I have to stay in shape.

- - -

The next morning came and I did my usual routine. Walking downstairs, I receive my tea as usual and greet Annie.

"Can you get me the files of everyone coming today?" I ask Annie politely. I usually order, but today I am in a good mood, I guess.

"Of course, darling, I'll go get them." She replied and leave.

Gus runs to me and licks me. Honestly, I can't get enough of him. This is probably the only man I love after my father.

That reminds me, I need to visit their graves today after the interviews.

I walk again around the house to inspect. I don't do that every day, so that I don't make everyone stay on alert. As much as I love people fearing me, I don't like seeing it every day.

"What's for lunch today Ezekiel?" I ask.

"Chicken Alfredo." He replies with a smile. He knows this dish is my favorite.

"Good." I nod and leave.

As for breakfast, I told him to make the same as yesterday, and don't worry, we do not throw food. In fact, the amount Ezekiel makes is for everyone in the house.

Just so you know, I eat my breakfast at 9, lunch at 2, and dinner at 7.

I walk back to the living room to find Annie standing with the files in her hand. I take them and sit on the couch.

I first open the secretary files.

•Amanda Cruise, 22, Canadian. She has 1-year experience working at Loke industries. She has no husband nor a kid.

•Isabelle Romano, 25, Italian. She has 3 years experience working at a local law firm. She has no husband nor a kid.

Great. One of them works at my enemy's company, so I don't have many options but to accept the other.

"You're sure you didn't find more?" I ask.

"No, I tried." She replies and I nod.

I open the other files.

•Jackson Still, 28, American. He used to work as a personal bodyguard for Lady Gaga. He has a wife and a baby.

•George Harlem, 34, American. He is a gym trainer. No wife or kid.

•Alessandro Esposito, 33, British. An ex-soldier. No wife but has a baby girl.

"Interesting" I say as soon as I read everyone's information.

"I will try to find more." Annie says.

"Just find me a secretary, I am not sure I'll like any of these. As for a personal bodyguard, I think I already chose one of these." I say.

"Okay darling."

—

The clock rolled to 3 and no one showed up yet.

I hate waiting.

"Where are they." I groan.

"They must be on their way, just calm down." Annie softly says.

As if on cue, the doorbell rings and Annie makes her way towards the door. I am sitting in my office to interview each one individually.

My door opens and Annie tells me that Amanda Cruise is here. I tell her to let her enter.

"Ms. Ferrari, it's so nice to meet you." The girl smiles a bit too much for my liking.

"So, Amanda, tell me, why do you want to work here?" I ask curiously.

"Honestly, I wanted to work here a long time ago, but you weren't hiring, but I am glad you are now." She excitedly says.

I cringe.

I give her the fakest smile, "And?"

"And?" She asks, clearly confused.

"What else, tell me. For example, where did you work before and why did you quit?" I ask even though I know the answer.

"I used to work at Loke industries, I like it there, but as I said, I wanted to work here in the first place." She nervously says.

I don't like her at all. First, she smiles too much, it's irritating. Second, she doesn't understand my question and clearly doesn't know how to answer. All in all, she's dumb.

"Unfortunately, Ms. Cruise, I don't want to work with you." I say bluntly.

"What?" She gasps.

"Did I stutter?" I glare at her. I hate to repeat what I had said.

"Leave. Now." I growl and she quickly stands up and leaves with tears running down her face.

Annie quickly enters the room with a questioning look.

"She's too clingy and a fan. I hate it." I grumbled.

After few seconds, Isabella enters the room.

"Ciao, Ms. Ferrari." She professionally greets with a nod.

(Hi)

I nod back.

"It says here you have 3 years experience at a law firm, am I correct?"

"Si, ma'am."

(Yes)

"Good, so tell me, why do you want this job and why did you quit that law firm?" I ask.

"To be honest with you, I need this job because I couldn't find another. I had to quit the law firm because.... because a man sexually assaulted me. I couldn't take it anymore and left."

"Why didn't you file a complaint if you don't mind me asking?"

"I did, but they wouldn't believe me, they believed him." She sadly says.

"Okay, Isabella. I would like to work with you and give me the man's name."

"Thank you so much! You will not regret it—and his name is Richard Stevenson." She replies and I nod.

I will make sure you don't see the light of day Richard Stevenson.

"I want to see you here at 9a.m sharp. If you're late, you're fired." I firmly say and she nods.

Good, I got my secretary.

Annie walks in and tells me that she's going to call the first guy, but I tell her to get me Alessandro, as I do not want to waste my time with the other. I also tell her to let the others leave.

Alessandro walks in and my eyes wandered from the top to the bottom.

His blonde hair and blue eyes. His thick yet decent biceps. His amazing body that could crush you with one touch...amazing.

"Mr. Esposito, have a seat."

"Ms. Amalia." He nods.

He called me Amalia...and for the first time I didn't mind, but he doesn't need to know that.

"Call me by my last name." I say firmly and he nods again.

"So, tell me Alessandro, why work here in Italy?"

"Well, my ex-wife lives here, and she has the custody of our daughter. I have to stay here to see her." He replies honestly.

I like his honesty.

"And why work as a personal bodyguard?" I ask, with amusement.

"To be honest, it's good money."

"And you want to work here to take the custody of our daughter?" I ask curiously.

"Yes, ma'am."

He is honest, responsible, would do anything for his daughter, which means, he will do anything for this job. He needs me as much as I need him.

"Fine—be here at 9a.m sharp. We will talk about how this is going to go and everything—by the way, where do you live?"

"An hour away from here." He replies, scratching the back of his neck.

"That's not good. When you come tomorrow, bring everything with you—you are going to live here."

"Sorry but that won't work. I have to have my own place" He says, making me furrow my eyebrows.

"Why?"

"I mean, if I want to win the custody of my daughter, I have to have my own home."

Ohhh

"Right. Then I'll find you an apartment near my place." I say with a smile.

A smile that I don't give too often. Tell me why did I give it again?

"I really appreciate that Ms. Ferrari, but I prefer to stay there." He replies bluntly.

"I totally understand, but it all comes with the job Alessandro. You have to live close to me and either way, do not worry about the rent. I pay it. I also pay my secretary's rent, so don't worry, it's nothing personal." I say, even though I didn't want to pay it just because it comes with the job, it's for his little girl.

"Fine, thank you Ms. Ama-Ms. Ferrari." He says, quickly realizing his mistake.

"See you tomorrow." I say and he nods and leaves.

-

I hope you like the first chapter of La Regina del Palazzo!

I really liked this chapter. I felt Amalia's power through the screen! I have always wanted to write a story like this. I mean... I haven't seen a lot of stories that show how important women are and how powerful they are!

Also! I know Amalia can be a real bitch, but...I kinda still like her

Please do not forget to vote and leave a comment! It really means a lot <3

Word count: 3330

# 2. The Handsome Bodyguard

Annie ^^^——

AMALIA

Tears.

Something I've always hated to see. I don't like to see someone crying or even me crying. I hate crying in general.

The last time I've cried was when my parents died and that was ten years ago, when I was fifteen.

Crying is for weak people.

If I saw someone crying in front of me, I would get mad, so mad. Annie told me that I feel that way because I don't want to remember the ugly night that took my parents away from me. That I don't cry because if I did, I won't stop.

Maybe she's right, maybe she isn't. There is nothing wrong with crying as long as you don't cry in front of me.

That excludes kids and babies of course.

Placing the bouquets on their graves, I kneel and pray for them. My parents. My life. I remember them...every single thing about them, especially the day and the way they died.

And do you know what's the worst part? is that I still don't know who's behind their death.

"I hope you are in a better place. I miss you so much. I am sorry I haven't been here in a while, but um...." I say out-loud, "-I have a lot of work, not that it's more important than you, but it's just urgent." I lied.

I don't know if they hear me, but I cannot show them that I am still broken for their death. I cannot make them believe that I am not happy.

Standing up, I make my way to the car to leave. I visit my parents every month, once or twice. It's not that I don't want to visit them every day, it's just I can't handle seeing them every day. Underneath that rock. That's why I lie to them every time I come here.

I may be heartless, emotionless, manipulative bitch, but when it comes to my parents, I am not those things.

Checking my watch, the clock turns 6. One hour left for dinner.

I walk inside the mansion and make my way to my room. I must freshen up before dinner.

I undress and remove my makeup. I take a quick shower and dress again. I don't know why I cannot wear pajamas in front of everyone in the house. I mean...it is my house, right? but still, I feel vulnerable.

Yes, I feel vulnerable when I wear pajamas in front of strangers.

Making my way downstairs, I walk to the dining room. The food is already on the table and so is Annie, waiting for me.

"Scusa, sono in ritardo." I say as soon as I sit.

(Sorry, I am late.)

"nessun problema caro."

(No problem, dear.)

I make my way to the head of the table and sit on the chair. I glance at Annie and know that she has something to say.

"If you have something to say, say it." I say, picking up the glass of water and sipping, waiting for her response.

"Are you okay?" She hesitantly asks. She already knows that I don't like to be asked these type of questions; a sentimental one, yet she still asks.

"I am fine." I simply reply. I know she is not satisfied with my answer, but I don't care.

I start eating the dinner Ezekiel made, which is Mushroom Risotto, one of my least favorites. I am not that picky about food and so, I don't give Ezekiel a list of foods to make, I just trust him and eat whatever he makes.

He is also one of the few people I trust after Annie and Gus. I trust him enough not to put poison in my food and kill me.

I glance at Annie again and caught her staring at me, with pity.

"You do this every time I visit their graves, why?" I ask firmly, clearly irritated with the way she's acting.

"Because I know that you are trying so hard not to show how sad you are—I don't want you to keep everything in and bury it inside of you." She explains.

"Annie, as much as I love you and understand your intentions, my life in none of your business, and so are my feelings." I finalize and stand up to leave. My appetite is gone.

"If you keep pushing everyone away like this, you are going to end up alone!" She yells, slamming her hands on the dining table.

I see one of the maids eavesdropping; Serena. She did not see me looking at her, yet.

"Well, Annie, what if I want to be alone?" I raise my left brow, waiting for her answer.

"You don't." She firmly says.

I am now so irritated and not in the mood to complete this nonsense conversation. I decide to leave to my room. Everyone is going to leave in an hour, so I'll come down when they do.

I walk towards the stairs, but before I go up, I say, "Serena—"

"Yes, ma'am?" She walks towards me, acting as if she came from the kitchen.

"You are fired." I say and walk up.

Entering my room, I undress and wear my comfy silk pajamas. I remove my makeup for the second time and walk towards the bathroom to do my night skin routine.

We should really take care of our skin, especially now that I am 25 years old, I must take care of it very well.

I jumped on the bed and hugged Gus, who was already snoring softly.

Gus and I have this ritual where the first to sleep must be hugged by the second. I don't know how he understood it or learned to do it, but I know that he's a smart little boy.

Maybe he is the only one that I don't hide my feelings from. I show him compassion, love, kindness, and give him multiple kisses. Something I don't do often to anyone but him.

I closed my eyes and welcomed darkness, and all I could think about is how excited I am for tomorrow.

Why?

I don't know.

——

The next morning, I woke up on the wrong side of the bed, which means, my mood was really really bad. I don't know why.

I get up from my bed and looked around for Gus, but couldn't find him. He must've gone for a walk at the garden.

I took a quick shower and dressed for the day. I picked out a simple white elegant dress that reached almost below the knee.

I walk to my toilette and start applying my makeup. My makeup is pretty simple. It consists of concealer, bronzer, blush, mascara, and a lipstick; mostly nude.

Believe it or not, Annie was the one who taught me how to do my makeup. Back in the day, she was a professional makeup artist, but after a terrible accident, she couldn't work with her hands like before.

That's why I don't let her do anything here other than some office work that she could handle.

I let my hair down for the first time in a while and head downstairs. Annie was waiting for me as usual with my cup of tea.

"Bongiorno." She greeted.

"Bongiorno—did Isabella arrive?" I ask quickly, trying to avoid the tension between us from yesterday's conversation.

"Yes, she is in the living room waiting for you."

Good.

Yesterday, Antonia was supposed to arrive at 8:30am instead of 9:00am because she was supposed to give me some files that I needed at the time, that's why I kicked her, but now for Isabella, she arrived just on time, maybe even before.

I nod and take the tea from her hand, and walk to the dining room to have my breakfast.

"Let her come to the dining room."

I take my seat and wait impatiently for the young lady, who is actually my age, but to me, she's young. The brain part I mean.

I know...I know, I shouldn't judge a book by its whatever, but I know people, I know them with just one look.

"Good morning, Ms, Ferrari." She greets professionally like the first time.

"Have a seat."

"Amalia, Alessandro Esposito is here." Annie says.

I dismissed the fact that he came in late because I know he lives far from here, but I still didn't like it.

"Okay, make him wait in the living room."

I start eating my breakfast and motion for Isabella to do too.

"So Isabella, tell me about yourself." I ask, even though I could care less about her life. I don't really care, but I just want to know some things.

"Well, I am single. My parents live in Florence with my brother—I came here to look for a job and you know...I found one at the law firm—yeah, that's about it."

"Any boyfriends?" I ask curiously. The last thing I need is a boyfriend, who will demand some free time from her, and I want her 24/7.

"No, I don't have one."

"Good."

"Now, let's talk about work—as you know, I run a company; a very successful one, and I choose my employees carefully, so you should consider yourself lucky. I hate laziness, a lot. I hate insufficient work, and I expect from you to be free 24/7. I might call you in the middle of the might and you have to answer. In my company, dating is forbidden, as well as, sleeping around—not that I am saying you would do that, but just informing you. Do you think you can handle it?"

"Yes, ma'am, I can and I will." She smiled brightly and I liked her confidence.

"Good—now, go to Annie and she will inform one of the drivers to drive you to the company. There is a file in my office that needs to be revised carefully; it's a contract. You would know since you worked in a law firm. So, your first assignment is to find any loopholes, any mistakes, or anything that looks suspicious."

"Okay, gracias Ms. Ferrari." She replies and gets up to leave.

I haven't even touched my food yet and she finished hers.

I called Annie to let Alessandro in. After few seconds, he strolls in.

"Greetings." He says with his strong and beautiful British accent.

I just nod.

"Please, eat." I invite him for breakfast, but he declines.

"You don't eat breakfast?" I ask, frowning.

"No it's not that, but I had breakfast with my daughter before I came in here." He explains.

"That's why you were late."

"Ahh-yes, it won't happen again."

"It better not." I reply firmly.

"So, let's talk about business." I start off before drinking my orange juice.

"The reason I hired a personal bodyguard is because I am a target. Someone or some people are trying to kill me and I need you to protect me."

"Why only one?" He asks curiously.

"Because I only need one to protect me Alessandro—indeed, they say the more the merrier, but I do not believe in that."

"You are right actually. Many bodyguards attract attention. It doesn't really matter how many you have because at the end, only one will protect you."

"Yes, exactly. However, I do have some bodyguards that come with my when I go out, but they are just two, and they annoy me, so it's good you are here."

"I don't annoy you?" He asks, and for some reason, I felt that we are getting to know each other and I don't like it.

But, I have to in order to trust him. I have to know him.

"No, you weirdly don't."

"By the way, did you bring your suitcase?"

"Yes, I did." He nods.

"Good because I have rented a house for you very close to mine. We can go there after breakfast."

Why do I feel that I have been having breakfast for hours?

"Thank you ma'am." He nods professionally and for some reason, it annoys me.

I finally finish my breakfast and stand up to leave, with him following me.

We walk into the living room and there were some maids cleaning. The moment they saw Alessandro, they froze up as if they saw the most beautiful man on Earth—not that he isn't.

My mood is already fucked up and they fucked it even more.

"Leave." I say harshly.

When they left, Annie walked in.

"Amalia, I sent Isabella to the company." She informs me.

"Thank you mamma." I nod gratefully. I glance at Alessandro to find him looking surprised.

Either with the fact that I for once acted nice or because Annie is my mother.

"Alessandro, meet Annie, my mother." I introduce him to Annie.

I know he saw her before, but I have to introduce them to each other, especially that he is going to be one of my most trusted people. Maybe.

I just hope he deserves the place.

"It's a pleasure ma'am." He shakes her hand.

"The pleasure is all mine." She replies and I roll my eyes.

"Annie, I am going to the company, I'll see you at lunch."

"Okay dear, take care."

Alessandro and I left the mansion and the driver took us to my company, but before that, we went to the apartment I rented for Alessandro.

"Do you like it?" I ask with a little excitement.

"Yes, a lot. My daughter will love it, thank you." He smiles for the first time and it bewitched me.

"Good."

It seems like I don't have another word other than 'good.' God...I am so bad at this. Whatever this is.

We shortly left the apartment and made our way to the company.

My company is a travel company, and I couldn't be more proud of it. Rich people mostly buy tickets to travel through us, and sometimes we give free tickets to the poor. Actually we do it often.

"Does you ex-wife and daughter live here in Sicily?" I ask.

"Yes."

"That's weird." I mumbled.

"Why is that? If you don't mind me asking ma'am."

Stop calling me ma'am! I am younger than you.

"Sicily isn't usually a city that is suitable for 'kids.' I mean...it's too dangerous."

"I know, but Amanda is stubborn. She wants to live beside her parents, and clearly she doesn't care."

Amanda...

"I see."

The car finally stopped and we stepped out, making our way inside the company. The moment I stepped in, the entire floor froze up.

Am I that scary?

"Am I that scary?" I find myself asking Alessandro.

I know I shouldn't trust him and talk to him freely that soon, but my gut tells me that he is trustworthy and good.

And my gut is always right.

"To them, yeah." He replies.

He is too honest, and I like it.

"And to you?" I ask as I walk into the elevator with him following me.

"No."

"Why not?"

"Let's just say, I have seen worse."

Does he mean that I am bad and that he had seen worse?

I wish I could fire him.

"You know I am your boss right?" I frown, receiving a chuckle.

Is he for real?

I was about to give him a piece of my mind, when the elevator opened.

I walk out, nodding at Isabella, who seemed to know what she's doing.

I enter my office and place my bag on my desk.

"Do you want to drink something?"

"No, thanks ma'am."

Ma'am. Fuck you.

I called Isabella to come to my office. 10 seconds and she was here.

"So, I know you just came a little while ago, but how do you find the work? Did you find the file I told you about?" I ask as I look around my desk, searching to see if the file is here or not.

"I am adjusting, and yes, I found it and I am working on it." She replies without hesitation.

"Found anything?"

"Not yet, no."

"Okay, you can leave."

She nodded and left, but not before glancing at Alessandro and giving him a smile, that he didn't return.

Good.

I sit behind my desk and start replying to some important emails. I ordered a coffee for myself, and water for Alessandro.

Since he doesn't want to drink anything, I figured he would at least want to drink water.

A couple of minutes later, I hear a knock.

"Come in."

Joseph; one of my employees, enters the room and places the tray of coffee and water on my desk.

"Thanks, Joseph."

"Your welcome, Ms."

Joseph is a very kind old man. He has been working here for as long as I could remember. He is a very trustworthy man and I would do anything for him. He is not on my list of 'people I trust' because we are not close and I don't consider him family.

"You can sit, you know."

"I am good, ma'am."

"Could you stop calling me ma'am?" I said a bit harshly, but didn't mean to.

He irritated me.

"Then what do you want me to call you?"

"I don't know, something else—Like Ms. for example."

"Fine, Ms."

Oh god, that's worse.

I just roll my eyes and focus my attention on the screen in front of me. Every few minutes, I would glance at Alessandro who is sitting on the couch, scrolling on his phone.

I don't know how people nowadays use their phones 24/7. I don't even know how to use it that well. I hate it, even despise it. It wastes time and is not good for your eyes.

After about half an hour, I hear a phone ring. I look up and saw Alessandro looking at me nervously.

"Your phone should be on silent, Alessandro." I say firmly, clearly irritated.

"Sorry, it's just my daughter. I'll just hang up." He quickly replies but I stop him.

"No, you can answer if it's your daughter..." I say quickly enough before he clicked decline.

He just nodded with a small smile and accepted the call.

"Ciao! Daddy!" A voice giggled.

"Hello, baby, how are you?" He replies with excitement.

"I miss you." She sadly replies.

For some reason, my heart fluttered. I don't know what it is, but I have a soft spot for children. I cannot say no to them, and I cannot yell or be mean to them. They are too pure and innocent for this world, and the last thing I want to do is to make them be someone like me, or worse...like him.

I hate this. I hate emotional moments, that's why I don't like to be surrounded by them. They always remind me of the past.

"I miss you too, pumpkin—I will see you this weekend."

"I am so excited to see our new home, daddy!"

I like how she used 'our' instead of 'your' as if she's moving in with her father forever, not going back to her mother's.

I wonder what her mother is like...

I wonder what Alessandro saw in her.

"I am excited for you to see it as well, baby—I will talk to you later, okay? I have work."

"Okay, daddy, tell your boss not to let you work a lot, okay?"

"Okay." He chuckles and hangs up.

"Sorry about her." He says nervously, placing his phone in his right pocket.

"It's fine." I reply

---

Walking into the kitchen, I see Ezekiel designing the plate. He looks so focused, so that he doesn't make any mistake.

"What's for lunch, Ezekiel?" I ask just in time for my stomach to make a sound.

"Fiorentina Steak." He replies excitedly as always.

"Okay, great." I smile and leave.

I finally changed my vocabulary!

I walk to the living room to find Annie and Alessandro talking, but stop when they see me. I narrow my eyes at them, feeling like they are hiding something, but of course I will not question it.

"Amalia, Mr. Stone called on the main phone and asked if he could come tomorrow for dinner. He has some business to speak with you." Annie informs me and I immediately scowl.

"Did he say what he wants to talk about?"

"No, he didn't."

"Fine, tell him he could come."

Tomorrow is Saturday, which means that Alessandro will not be here. As much as I want him to stay 24/7 here, he has a daughter to see, so I gave him permission to go on the weekends to the house I rented for him, to stay with his daughter, since he could only see her on weekends.

"Ms. Ferrari, if you need me here tomorrow, I could stay." Alessandro says, referring to when Jeremy comes tomorrow.

"No, it's fine. I could take care of it—besides, you have to be with your daughter."

I walk to my room and sit on the bed. It's 1:30PM, which means 30 minutes left till dinner. I could take a quick nap, right?

As I put my head on the pillow, I find myself thinking about Alessandro. Not in a romantic way, but more like thinking about his life. Why did he leave the military? Why did he divorce his wife?

I mean, I know it is not my business, but I must know everything about my employees, especially when he is someone that will be close to me 24/7.

The 30 minutes passed, and I did not sleep. I was thinking a lot that I forgot to sleep.

Walking to the dinning room, I find Annie and Alessandro sitting on the table. The maids are putting the food on the table and I didn't miss the way they are looking at Alessandro.

When I entered, the maids froze and acted professionally. For some reason, they fear me...and I think they should.

I sit on my seat and gesture for the rest to start eating.

Whilst eating, I start a conversation.

"Alessandro, you could go tonight to your house, in case your daughter comes early in the morning."

He looks at me with a confused look, as if he is trying to figure out why I am deeply concerned about his daughter.

I just love kids...

"Thank you." He nods and continues to eat.

"Umm Amalia..." Annie starts, and I immediately know she's about to say something bad.

"Patricia called."

"Don't say her name in this house." I scowl at her. She knows I can't stand to hear that name, yet she still says it.

"She's your sister Amalia, you have to talk to her." That made my chuckle.

Sister.

What an ugly word for an ugly person.

"She probably needs money." I laugh humorlessly.

"It's different this time, Amalia. Just please, talk to her." She pleads.

"That's enough mamma!" I snap, "I will not speak with that betraying bitch!" I yell, tears prickle at the corners of my eyes, but I did not dare let them run down.

I will not cry about them ever again, ever.

I don't usually yell at Annie, in fact, I never yell, but sometimes I cannot control my anger.

I glance at Alessandro to find him looking at me with a clenched jaw. Of course, he is like everyone. He thinks that I don't respect my own mother and I treat everyone badly. He thinks I am dramatic.

It's not that I don't respect Annie, I do. But sometimes, she crosses to line and it angers me. I know a mother never crosses the line with her children, but she knows I will act this way when she brings up my sister, yet she still does.

I am breathing heavily. I couldn't concentrate on anything. My mother is on the verge of crying and I didn't want that. I can't let her cry.

"Mi dispiace, mamma." I say sincerely (I am sorry, Mom).

"It's okay, il mio bambino. You are right." She looks down sadly (My baby).

"Per favore, stop bringing her up." (Please)

"Never again." She nods.

I stand up to leave, making my way out of the dining room. Passing the kitchen, I hear some maids talking.

"He is so handsome. I wish I could kiss him right now." One says.

"I know right! The things he would do to my body..." The second replies dreamily.

"Too bad he is stuck with the devil herself." The first one says disgustingly.

"I am sure she will sleep with him in no time—just like she slept with Jeremy Stone."

"Oh my god! She did?"

"Yes!"

It's time to let them know I heard them. I enter the kitchen and the moment they saw me, their faces paled.

"M-Ms. Ferrari, h-how can I help you?"

"Nothing, just wanted to let you know that you are fired." I smile brightly. A fake smile of course.

"Oh and—I will make sure you don't get a job here in Sicily, ever." I added and left.

---

I hope you liked this chapter!!!

I know nothing exciting happened! but this chapter gives away a little bit of Amalia's past. What do you think happened between her and her sister; Patricia? And what do you think happened to Amalia's parents? She said they were killed, but what do you think?

Also, are you excited for Alessandro's daughter to meet Amalia? Do you think she will like her?

Word count: 4245

# 3. The Midnight Thief

LILY^^^

AMALIA

It's midnight and Alessandro left to his new house. As I said, I sent him early in case his daughter came in early in the morning.

For some weird reason, I am excited to meet his daughter. I wonder if she looks like him or like his mother. I haven't really seen how Amanda looks like. I hope she looks like Alessandro.

It just dawned to me that Alessandro's name is Italian, and I wonder if either of his parents is Italian. It had to be his father because he has an Italian family name as well, but still, I want to ask him.

Adjusting my head on the pillow, I close my eyes to welcome sleep. I am so tired and I am really not looking forward for tomorrow. Not only I am not in the mood to see Jeremy Stone, but also, I am not in the mood to see Annie. I know I shouldn't say that, but after today, I really don't want to talk to her for a while.

Suddenly, I hear a voice coming from downstairs. I don't normally hear anything because of how big my mansion is, but it was close. So close.

I hear it again and I get a feeling of uneasiness. What if something happened to Annie?

Where is Gus?

I look around and don't find him. As if on cue, I hear him bark.

I quickly wore my red silky robe and walk downstairs, snatching my phone with me in the process.

I prepare Alessandro's number, but don't dial it.

I have many guards, it can't be someone breaking in, right? It never happened.

I arrive at the living room and saw Gus unconscious kn the floor.

"Gus!" I yell and run to him.

I try to wake him up, but he doesn't. I check to see if he's still breathing and thank god he is.

I click 'call' and wait for Alessandro to pick up.

Before I could do anything, I see a shadow emerging from one of the rooms, with what seem a bag on their shoulder.

I leave the phone on the floor and quickly stand up and pick up something to defend myself with.

I picked up a vase.

The shadow starts walking towards the living room, tiptoeing, making sure no one hears.

Whatever he took, I cannot let him leave with it. From what I know, the room he emerged from is my collection room.

Sometimes, I buy vintage stuff and collect them in my room.

They are extremely expensive.

"Stop right there!" I yell, holding the vase close to me.

The shadow stops and turns towards me. It seemed he is a man because of how he is built. I can't see his face because of the mask he has on.

He puts his bag on the floor and takes something out of his pocket.

A gun.

"Don't make me use it, woman." He says dangerously.

"I dare you!" I hiss. I was playing with fire, but I don't care.

No one and I mean no one can threaten me.

"Leave before you see something you don't like—without the bag of course." I say firmly.

"Stupid." He chuckles and makes his way towards me.

"You women are you stupid—I have a gun, can't you see?" He chuckles again.

"I see—" I say back with a smirk, "—I don't know how you got rid of my guards, but there is someone you didn't get rid off, and he's standing right behind you."

The man immediately turns around and saw Alessandro standing there aiming his gun at him.

Everything after that happened fast. The man wrapped his arm around my neck and aimed his gun at me.

"Let me go or I kill her." The thief growls.

I know a killer when I see one, and this thief is not a murderer.

"Leave her before I empty this gun on you." Alessandro's low and dangerous voice says.

He kept his firm hold on me and tightened it a little bit, making it hard to breathe.

I want to do something to break free, but I decided against it. For some wicked reason, I want to see what will Alessandro do. It's not that I can do something anyways because he had his gun aimed at me.

The thief starts walking backwards with me trailing behind him. Suddenly, a voice screams.

"Oh my god!" Annie emerges, standing next to Alessandro.

"Mama, go to your room." I struggle to say because of how tight this man's arm around my neck.

Alessandro says something to her and she leaves.

"One more move and I will shoot!" Alessandro barked, still aiming the gun at him.

The thief did not listen and Alessandro apparently wasn't lying when he said that because the next thing I see is the thief on the floor with blood oozing out of his arm.

I could have avoided all that if I just broke free, but I didn't.

I am a really bad person.

But then again, he had his gun pointed at me and he's a thief, he deserves it.

I quickly break free, making sure to take the gun from the thief's hand, and run to Alessandro.

The thief was groaning from pain, clutching his arm dearly.

Out of nowhere, policemen enter the living room, searching for the intruder. Once they saw him on the floor, they picked him up and took him away.

"Are you okay?" Alessandro says, cupping my cheeks.

I don't like this.

"Il mio bambino!" Annie sobs, entering the living room and hugging me.

I hug her back.

"I am okay, mamma."

"When did this happen? Where were the guards?" She fires questions whom answers I don't know.

"I don't know mamma, but I will get to the bottom of this." I reply.

I glance back at Alessandro and smile at him.

"Thanks for coming as soon as you could."

"When you called and didn't talk, I heard voices and I immediately felt something was wrong—and no problem."

Suddenly, my mind goes to Gus. I glance at his still unconscious body and kneel in front of him.

"Baby—wake up." I try to wake him up, but he doesn't budge.

I think the thief gave him some type of syringe or something and injected him with it.

"Can you please carry him to my room?" I ask Alessandro.

He nods and walks to me to pick him up.

I motion for him to follow me, so I could lead him to my room.

I can't believe he will see my room now.

Opening the door, I stroll in with him following. He places my baby on the bed and I cover Gus with the duvet.

As much as it pains me to thank someone for doing his damn job, I feel I have to.

"Grazie Alessandro." I softly say.

"Prego, Amalia." He replied and my breath hitched.

This is the second time he calls me Amalia, but the difference is that this time he did it intentionally, why? Who knows, but this time I didn't correct him.

"You can leave." I nod gratefully.

"I don't think I can leave you and Annie without protection, especially that the guards are nowhere to be seen."

"But, you have to be home for your daughter." I frown.

I want him to stay.

"She won't come alone in the morning, if anything, Amanda will be with her. She can call me."

Amanda?

"Oh, so Amanda is also coming." I say as I look somewhere at the ceiling.

"She's just driving her." He explains and I nod.

"Okay, you can sleep in the guest room."

"I'd rather sleep here at the chair if you don't mind. I don't think leaving you is the right thing to do, and Annie is next door I believe, so she's close."

I guess he knew where's her bedroom because she came up with us when we carried Gus to my room.

"I...Don't mind." I finally say.

I don't like him staying here, but I want to. Do you know what I mean?

It's like I want to, but my mind doesn't want to admit it, but I want to.

Oh god...I am starting to get crazy! All because of his handsome face.

I wonder how he doesn't remember me...

It's a long story, but to summarize, three days ago was not the first day Alessandro and I meet. I have met him years ago, yet he doesn't seem to remember me.

He walks to the comfy chair and sits, but not before taking off his jacket.

I eye him warily and slide under the covers, without removing my jacket. I am only wearing a short red silky dress and I don't intent for him to see it.

I hug Gus and try ti sleep, but my mind was overthinking and all I could think about is Alessandro.

I open my eyes and glance at him, only to find him looking at me. Our eyes locked and none of us look away.

I couldn't anymore and I averted my gaze.

I close my eyes again feeling extremely safe because Alessandro is here.

For some unknown reason, I wish he's in my bed right now.

——

"I am coming baby, just give me five minutes—wait with your mom." I hear a voice say.

I slowly open my eyes to see Alessandro wearing his jacket. I look around and find Gus walking into my room and a smile spread on my lips.

"Baby! I am so sorry." I walk to him and hug him tightly.

Suddenly, I remember that Alessandro is here and he saw this side of my that I don't show to anyone other than Gus.

"You'r leaving?" I ask him.

"Yes, my daughter just called."

"What's her name by the way?"

"Lily. Her name is Lily."

Lily...

"Okay—thanks again and enjoy."

"Thanks Ms."

Are we back to Ms.?

I just roll my eyes.

He leaves my bedroom and I walk to my bathroom. I take a quick shower, scrubbing my body very well. I din't want that man's filthy hands to stay any longer on my body even if he just touched my neck.

I apply my shampoo and conditioner and wash them off.

I wrap a towel around my body, and exit the bathroom.

What should I wear today? I have to look good.

I walk to my walk-in closet and glance at the dresses that are hanged.

Red, blue, or white?

I decide on wearing the blue dress. It was a mid-thigh blue dress that has a small slit on the right side, and thin straps. I paired it with light nude heels.

I put my hair down for the second time now, and apply a little bit of makeup.

Walking downstairs, I receive my tea.

"Morning mamma, slept well?"

"Hello baby, yes and you?"

"Like a baby."

Today is Saturday, which means no work and no Isabella. Also, all my staff were sent home, only Ezekiel is here.

"What's for breakfast Ezekiel?"

"Omelettes." He replies and I just nod.

"Annie, make sure to tell Ezekiel to prepare a dinner for the four of us, okay."

By four I mean, Jeremy, Annie, Ezekiel, and I.

"Yes, don't worry."

I walk to the backyard and see Gus playing with a random cat.

What the hell?

"My baby is growing up." I murmured.

"He never played with a cat, I wonder what changed." Annie comments.

"What if he's dying and trying to make amends with everyone? Oh my god!" She adds and I roll my eyes.

"If he's dying, I'd know first."

"Why would he make amends with you?"

"Not amends mamma, but he is obsessed with me and will not leave me for even a second." As soon as I said that, Gus came walking towards me and starts licking my arm.

"Baby!" I coed and start petting him.

"Amalia..." Annie starts and from her tone, I know I won't like what she's going to say next. I just hope she doesn't mention my sister again.

"I want to see your kids."

What?

"Ha?" I frown, "—kids?" I chuckle, putting my newspaper down.

"Yes, your kids Amalia. I want to see you get married and have kids of your own. I want you to become a mother." She says and a tear rolls down onto her cheek.

"Where is this coming from mamma?" I ask.

She knows very well that I will never get married nor have kids of my own.

"Every mother wants to see her children happy and married."

"I don't have to get married and have kids to be happy, mother." I say firmly, annoyed that she opened this conversation all together.

"You are going to be a great mother, il mio bambino." She smiles and wipes her tears.

Again with that. How can she be so sure that I will be a mother, I won't!

"Yeah....yeah." I roll my eyes and pick up my newspaper again to see what's new.

Jeremy Richard Stone has been found dead in his home this morning. His daughter called the authorities after she woke up and found her father's dead body in his office. The authorities confirmed it's a murder when they found he'd been shot, with no murder weapon. An investigation bas been opened and the EISA is working on the case.

Shit.

I quickly stand up, dropping the newspaper on the floor.

"What happened?" Annie's voice says with panic.

"Jeremy Stone is dead."

He was supposed to come here for dinner. He wanted to tell me something. It must be too important that he got killed for it.

What did he want to tell me? I have to know, but how?

"What! How?"

"Someone murdered him." I reply and make my way inside.

Tomorrow is the weekly circle, I am certain it's one of the members.

"Where are you going?" Annie asks, trailing behind me.

"I have to see his family. I have to know if they know something the police doesn't."

"You can't go alone! The guy just got murdered. Take Alessandro with you." She yells.

"No. Alessandro is not working today and he is with his daughter. I cannot ask him to come with me."

"Don't go Amalia please!"

"I'll take some of the new bodyguards you recruited this morning, don't worry mamma." I kissed the top of her head, and left the mansion, motioning for two bodyguards to come with me.

"Guard this place with your lives." I order the rest and they nod approvingly.

I step into the jeep, along with the bodyguards and the driver. I give the driver the address and we speed off.

Driving the long street beside my mansion, we pass Alessandro's house. I look and found him walking with his daughter outside, but her face wasn't clear.

My eyes catch his and he sees me, and a frown covered his face. He signals for me to stop, but I don't.

The last thing I need is for someone to ask me questions.

Not in the mood.

—

"Hello Ms. Ferrari." Angelina's voice cracks as she speaks.

"Angelina, may your husband rest in peace." I give my condolences.

It's really hard for most people to not cry in these situations, but honestly, I feel nothing. Not because I don't care about Jeremy's death, but because...umm okay maybe because I don't care about his death, but not because I am heartless, it's because we weren't that close for me to cry over him.

Angelina lets me in and I sit beside the many people who are here to give their condolences.

I see his little girl; Sara, sitting on the chair and silently crying. She's a 15 years old young girl, who has no siblings. She's the only child.

She just lost her father the same age I lost mine, the only difference is that she has her mother.

I walk towards the girl and sit on the chair beside hers.

"Sara." I call and she looks up with her watery eyes, trying to make sense of who I am.

She never saw me before.

"I am your father's close work friend." I smile softly.

"Nice to meet you." She weakly says.

"I have to ask you something dear." I start, even though I want to stop myself from asking because it's not the time for that, but I have too.

"Yes?"

"I know you don't want to constantly remember what happened, but I have to know if you saw who did it?"

She looks confused at first and I feel that she wants to say something, but she decided against it.

"No, I didn't."

"Did you hear anything?"

"No." She replies harshly this time.

I got my message and stand up. The last thing I need is to make a scene right here and now. I say my goodbyes to Angelina and make my way out to my car.

The police were everywhere, making sure no one comes into the house without Angelina consent. It really sucks to live in your house that was supposed to be your safe place, yet live with fear of getting killed or something.

Stepping into the car, I order the driver to move. One of the bodyguards, who I still don't know his name, keeps eyeing me, and I don't like him.

"What's your name?" I ask harshly.

"Gino Ms."

"And you?" I ask the other, who seems rather shy.

"Donte ma'am." He replies shyly.

"You two will accompany me from now on, and you Gino, keep your eyes to yourself."

"Sorry Ms. I was just looking at the scar on your neck, it seems familiar."

How dare he!

I hide it with my hair and try to calm myself down.

"My scar is none of your business—don't push your limits." I finalize and step put of the car.

I make my way to the mansion and knock on the door.

Few seconds passed and the door opens revealing Annie. However, behind her is Alessandro and his little girl.

The moment my eyes meets hers and hers meets mine, we say in unison,

"You!?"

The fuck...

—

I hope you liked this chapter you guys!!!!

I really had fun writing it and I hope you liked it too.

What do you think of this chapter? Any theories?

Word count: 3079

# 4. Bonding

ISABELLA^^^—

AMALIA

Recap from the last chapter.

The moment my eyes meet hers, and hers meets mine, we say in unison,

"You!?"

The fuck...

------

"Nanny Amalia?" The young girl grins.

Nanny?

"Lily? Darling...what are you doing here?" I ask, clearly confused. Why is she holding Alessandro's hand?

Wait a second.

This Lily is his Lily?

Damn...

"How do you know my daughter?" He asks, narrowing his eyes. As soon as he asked me that question, my mind goes back to two weeks ago when I met this little girl.

FLASHBACK

"Annie, I am leaving." I say before opening the front door and step out. It's a beautiful Sunday morning, and the weather is just...rema rkable.

Stepping into the backseat, I order the driver to take me to my favorite little coffeeshop close to my company before heading there.

After few minutes, the car comes to a halt, and I step out and enter the shop.

"Welcome Ms. Ferrari, long time no see!" One of the waitresses greets.

"Hello Chloe." I greet back with a nod.

"The usual?" She asks and I nod.

This is the only coffee shop that makes a good Spanish Latte here in Sicily. I mean...I am a coffee lover and of course I have tried every coffee shop here, and trust me, none of them is as good as this one.

"Here you go Ms. Ferrari; I hope to see you soon." Chloe smiles, handing me the cup.

"Thanks Chloe." I mustered a small smile and handed her the money.

Walking outside the shop, I make my way to the car. As I was opening the door, I hear a loud cry. I quickly turn around and saw a little girl calling for her mother and sobbing hard.

I don't know what people would do in these situations. I don't see anyone approaching her, so I walk towards the little girl and kneel to her level.

"Hello sweetie, why are you crying?" I ask, even though I know she lost her mother somewhere in this road.

Anger starts to rise up within me at the thought that the mother is shopping somewhere, not caring if she lost her daughter.

Yet...her mother might also be looking for her.

"I lost my mother." She cries more. She appears to be 5 years old thank god because otherwise, I wouldn't understand a word she says.

She also speaks English...

"Where did you see her last?" I ask softly, grabbing her by the waist and pushing her softly towards me.

Motherly instincts I guess...even though I had never been a mother before.

"I was playing at that park—" She points at the park beside the café, "—and when I turned around, she wasn't there. She said something but I didn't here." A sob left her pretty mouth.

"Don't worry baby, I will take care of you until you find her, okay?" I smile warmly.

"Promise?"

"I promise."

I take her hand in mine and we walk towards the park. I keep looking inside the shops, hopping to see a woman who is freaking out for losing her child, but I don't.

"What does she look like?"

"She has brown hair..." She says, trying to remember more.

Suddenly, we hear a voice yell.

"Lily!" We turn around and found a woman, who appears to be in her late 20's, struggling to pick all of her shopping bags.

She walks towards us and looks up at me.

"What's going on?" She asks and my blood boils.

"Where were you mommy?" The girl; whose name is Lily, cries.

"I told you I was going to shop a little while you play!" She explains a little too loudly.

"How could you leave your little girl alone and go shopping?" I bark. Didn't mean to do that in front of Lily, but I couldn't stop myself.

"Who are you to question me? She is MY daughter!" She yells back, taking Lily's hand from my own.

"Well Ms., you don't want to know." I reply dangerously, "—take care of your daughter before it's too late."

"Get out of my face you bitch!" She yells and for the first time, my eyes widen. Not because I am taken aback, but because she said that in front of her daughter. She literally cursed in front of her daughter.

I glance at the little girl and see her looking at the floor. Is it from shame of having a mother like this? I don't know.

I don't say anything else, even though I want to so bad, but it's because of that little girl. I walk back to my car and speed off, but before all that, I whispered my name to the little girl, so she would remember me, always.

END OF FLASHBACK

"Amalia!" She giggles and runs towards me, hugging my legs.

I am in shock.

I hug her back and kneel to her level, giving her a kiss on the cheek.

"Amalia, how do you know my daughter?" Alessandro asks again, saying my name this time. Hallelujah!

"I met her a while back, before I met you." I reply broadly.

"Don't tell daddy I went missing." Lily whispers, earning a confused look from Alessandro. I just nod.

"Annie, could you take care of Lily for 5 minutes please?" Alessandro asks and she agrees. He motions for me with his hand, and we walk to the backyard.

"I am so confused right now, but first, why didn't you take me with you? You could've died there! What if someone killed you?" He starts yelling, clearly forgetting that I am that boss.

He looks at me, waiting for my answer and breathing so hard.

"Alessandro be careful to your tone and your words. I am not your friend." I say dangerously, "—secondly, I decide when you come with me, and not you." I added.

I don't know why he was angry or was yelling at me as if I am his girlfriend. What is he thinking?

"I am sorry...I just, I was worried." He says.

Of course, he was worried. Worried that I die and so does his job.

"Don't worry about your job Alessandro, even if I die, you are secured." I explain, making him frown.

"This is not about—"

"Daddy!" Lily cuts him off.

"Yes, sweetie?"

"Can we stay here? Please! I want to play with nanny Amalia." She pleads.

God...nanny? Really? Where did she get that from?

"No baby, we have to go home. Ms. Amalia wants to rest." He explains and she pouts. She looks at me with pleading eyes.

If you are in my position, would you say no? of course not! Especially to a kid.

"I believe I could fit you in my schedule, Lily." I give her a small smile.

"YES!" She jumps and hugs me. I stiffen a bit, not liking that Alessandro is seeing this side of me.

"You really don't have to do that..." He starts, but I shut him up with one of my glares.

Why does every parent say that? I mean first Ashelia and now Alessandro.

It's currently 6PM and Alessandro and his daughter are still here. Alessandro wanted to leave a long time ago, but his daughter wouldn't let him, and so, I told them to stay for dinner and then leave.

Thank god I don't have work today.

"Are you happy with your mom, Lily?" Alessandro asks his daughter. From his tone, I could tell that he knows she wouldn't be, but why?

"Yeah..." She hesitates a little bit. I glance at her and narrow my eyes. She shakes her head as a no, when she sees me looking at her.

"Is something wrong?" I ask this time.

"No, there is not. I just miss my dad." She replies, hugging her father.

"Do you have children nanny Amalia?" She asks, making Annie and I choke. Alessandro's eyes widen and scolds his daughter a bit.

"No, I don't." I try to smile.

"But why not? Does your husband not want kids?" She pushes more.

"Lily—" Alessandro warns, "—not everyone is married."

Gus comes running into the room saving me from Lily. Once Lily sees him, she jumps out of her father grasp and goes to play with him. Surprisingly, Gus likes her.

"I am sorry about her." Alessandro starts.

"It's fine, she's just a kid." I reply, looking everywhere but at him.

"Now tell me, how did you meet my daughter?" He asks in a serious voice.

I don't like when he questions me...god I want to kill him.

"We met at a park." I simply say.

"Elaborate."

"It's none of your business Alessandro." I groan.

"It is, she's my daughter."

"And I am your boss, so you listen to me."

"Tell me."

"Why don't you ask your ex-wife, I am sure she'll tell you."

"You met Amanda?"

"How else would I meet your daughter?" I ask confusedly. Is he crazy?

"She always lies, so I am not going to ask her."

"Alessandro stop, I am not going to tell you."

"But why?"

"Because it is between me and Lily. Only us."

"Something happened, am I right?"

"Something like what?" I ask, and just now I notice how close Alessandro and I are. We are so close.

"She lost her again, didn't she?"

Again!? WHAT THE ACTUAL FUCK

"Again?" I furrow my brows.

"So, she did?" He growls, putting his palms on his face.

"Calm down, thank god I found her." I mutter, trying to calm him down. For some reason, I feel like I am talking with my husband. What the hell? It has been only 3 days and Alessandro turned my life upside down.

This is NOT me!

"How could I calm down? What if one day I lose my daughter?"

"Why didn't you use this at the court?"

"They didn't believe me because there wasn't any proof, plus, I didn't want my daughter to testify."

"But, why didn't they believe you?" I ask curiously.

"because I was an ex-military. They thought I had mental proble ms.... you know from war, and so they thought it is better for the girl to stay with her mother."

"But, that's unfair."

"I know."

"Alessandro." I start and he hums in reply.

"Starting from Monday, I am your boss that you met on day 1. —no talking like this and no yelling like you did at the backyard, am I clear?"

"Yes, you are." He mutters and leaves the living room.

Am I, not right? I mean, I recruited him for a reason and that reason wasn't this. He is my bodyguard and that's it.

After dinner, the Esposito's left to their home, leaving me alone with Annie and Gus. As much as I like my space, I already miss Lily. She added something to this mansion that will never happen again. I don't know what it is, but I love her...deeply. I only met her once before today, and since that day, she has taken my heart.

Walking into my room, I take my clothes off, and make my way to the bathroom. I need to take a very long bath to relax my body.

I step into the bath and sit. My body instantly relaxes. I close my eyes and think about everything that had happened in the past couple of days.

My mind wanders to Alessandro. The first day I met him, I can't deny that I found him extremely attractive, I still do. His body...his mesmerizing eyes...the way he looks at me...makes me want to do so many things to him.

After the hot bath, I clean my hair and step out of the bathroom.

I go under the duvet after wearing my silky pajamas, and hug Gus tightly. Apparently, he came while I was taking a bath.

He groans a bit, signaling that he knows I am here, and goes back to sleep.

Gosh...I love him.

--------

Monday

Wearing my black dress and nude heels, I make my way downstairs. Isabella should be here any minute. If she's not, she's fired.

"Is Isabella here?" I ask Annie as I take my tea from her.

"Yes honey, and so is Alessandro." She replies, and for some reason, I didn't like what she told me.

I walk towards the living room and Isabella was talking to Alessandro and laughing. He was laughing too.

I clear my throat and they immediately stop laughing.

"Good morning Ms. Ferrari."

"Good morning."

I just nod and sit on the couch.

"Did you finish the file? if yes, did you find anything?" I fire my question at Isabella.

"Yes, I did—this contract is not very good Ms. If you signed it, there is a huge potential that you lose 1$ million dollars."

"And why is that?" I test her.

This contract is my doing. I invented it. I created it. This is just a test for Isabella, so I see her potential. Is she smart?

"Because if you decided to terminate this contract, they could sue you, and if they did, they will win because according to article 10 of this contract, you cannot terminate unless the other end want, which means, they could agree for terminating, and then use it to their advantage and sue you."

Mhm.

"Good, Isabella. You may leave." I look at her from under my lashes. Despite her annoying me this morning, she is a good employee.

"Thanks ma'am." She nods and leaves.

After she left, I look up and glance at Alessandro, who was looking straight. I want to have minimum contact with him today because after my sex dream yesterday, I don't think I could keep my hands to myself.

"We are leaving." I announce.

"Don't you want to eat breakfast?" Annie asks.

"My appetite is gone." I say as I glance at Alessandro, who was looking at me. A frown covers his beautiful face.

"Mamma, if you need anything, ask or take two bodyguards. Their names are Gino and Donte." I say.

"Who are they?" Alessandro immediately asks.

I just roll my eyes and keep walking to the car.

I could hear Annie telling him about the bodyguards. When I told him that starting from Monday, I would go back to being me, he probably thought I was joking. Now, I know he just asked a question, but as I said, I want to have minimum contact with him.

Stepping into the backseat, Alessandro follows me from the other side, and we speed off. I told the driver to stop first at my favorite coffee shop, since I haven't been there in a while.

"Did I do something wrong?" Alessandro suddenly asks.

"No, you didn't."

"then why are you not even looking at me?" He asks, clearly annoyed.

"Do I have to look at you?" I arch my brow, still not looking at him.

"Yes actually, you have to." He replies and I get angry. Who the hell does he think he is?

"What did I tell you when you were at my house two days ago, Alessandro?"

"That you are going to be like the first day you met me." He answers and I nod, "then why are you surprised?" I ask.

"Because the you now is not the you of the first day."

God this man!

"What do you want from me Alessandro?"

"Nothing, I want nothing." He replies and looks elsewhere.

"Spit it out, Alessandro.." I order, rolling my eyes.

"Lily wants me to take a picture with you." He quickly says, shocking me.

A picture with me?

"Why?" I frown.

"She likes you." He says, and that made me smile.

"Fine." I roll my eyes and get closer to him to take the damn picture.

"How are you going to send it?" I ask, narrowing my eyes.

"She is going to visit my mother's house, so I'll send it to my mother." He explains and I nod.

He takes out his phone and opens the camera. He comes a little closer to me and eventually puts his arm around my waist. I stiffened a bit, especially after my dream.

I didn't like it. Not one bit.

I try to smile, just for the little girl. His hand tightened around my waist for some reason, and I found comfort in that. Why? Who knows...

"I think two pictures would satisfy her." He chuckles.

"Yeah, I thi—" I was cut off by a loud bang.

The car stops to a halt and the next thing I hear is gunshots.

----

I hope you liked this chapter you guys!!!!

What do you think of it? I personally liked it and liked writing it as well! <3

Tell me your thoughts and theories <3

Also! Do you have any theories as to where Amalia met Alessandro? And tell me your thoughts on Lily, do you like her? I personally adore her

Don't forget to vote and comment you guys! It really means a whole lot

Also, don't forget to follow me on

Instagram @thesenoradenna

I will try as soon as I can to upload the next chapter! I will try my hardest to write it soon for you guys to read it

Word count: 2879

# 5. Glad You're Here

Recap:

"I think two pictures would satisfy her." He chuckles.

"Yeah, I thi—" I was cut off by a loud bang.

The car stops to a halt and the next thing I hear is gunshots.

——AMALIA

"What's going on?" I yell, as I press my hands on my ears. The noise was too loud for my liking.

"Stay down!" Alessandro yells and takes out his gun from his holster.

He then starts shooting from the window, targeting the attackers.

The driver is long dead. It's just me and Alessandro.

Suddenly, he takes my hand and pushed my forward. He opens the car door and we step out, but stay down. He shoots again hitting other two.

"When I say run, you tun. Understood?" He orders and I nod frantically.

"But what about you?"

"I will be behind bella." He replies and my breath hitches for calling me 'bella'

It's not the time Amalia!

Almost immediately, he yells, "RUN!"

I run as fast as I could the other way. I don't think I have ever ran like this before.

I look back to see that Alessandro isn't following me. I stop and my heart beats fast.

"Alessandro!"

"Run Amalia! RUN!"

I can't leave him. I can't leave him. I kept telling myself. But if I don't leave, we both could die and his efforts to save me would have gone for nothing.

I look back for the last time, seeing him shooting those attackers. There are four of them left and they are gaining on Alessandro. I cannot leave him.

I try to ignore the fear within me and a sudden confidence spread through me.

I walk towards one of the dead bodies and take a gun. Blood is everywhere and I feel sick. I want to vomit.

Controlling myself, I lay low and walk slowly towards Alessandro.

"What are you doing?" He barks.

"Don't you dare bark at me, I am your boss." I say firmly.

"This is not the time Amalia!" He yells and goes back to shooting.

I take out the gun I took from the bloody dead body, and shoot randomly hitting one of the four.

My luck is with me today I guess.

Alessandro turns towards me with a confused look. He thought I couldn't shoot—well he's not wrong, but I am just lucky.

He shoots again and the shooting stops.

I peek a little bit to find them all dead. I sigh in relief, dropping the gun.

"I can't believe this happened." I calmly say as I look straight.

"You should have ran, what if you died?" He yells and my blood boils. STOP YELLING!

"Nothing happened see—" I point at myself, "—in perfect shape."

"It's not funny Amalia, I am the one who is supposed to protect you, not the way around."

"What would I tell Lily if you died?" I ask and he shuts up.

There's a silence before he speaks up again.

"We need to maximize the security at your home, and when we go out as well."

"You're right—I bet when I go to the circle meeting tomorrow, they will be surprised that I'm alive."

"Are you sure it's one of them?" He asks as he looks into my eyes.

"So sure." I nod and stand up, giving him my hand to help him.

He takes my hand we stands up, rubbing his pants to remove any dirt.

"We need to leave before more come." He announces as he takes the driver's body outside the car. He gets in and I do too.

"Let's go home to freshen up."

——

Scrubbing the dirt from my body, I clean it with water and wash my hair.

I walk out of the bathroom with a robe wrapped around my body. I comb my hair swiftly, and walk to my walk-in closet to get ready.

I look between my dresses and blazers, and decide to wear a white blazer set. I haven't worn that in a hot minute.

I apply a little makeup, and spray my favorite perfume.

I walk downstairs and find Alessandro waiting for me with Annie.

"Are you okay sweetie?" She asks, worry is evident in her voice.

"I am mamma—I want to maximize the security here, and I want you to stay home and never leave for a while."

"I will get on to that." She nods, "—but be careful okay?"

"Don't worry mamma, Alessandro is with me." I smile as I look at him.

He smiles back. He smiles back!

I shake my head to get rid of some certain thoughts.

"You can go rest if you want." I tell Alessandro as I walk into the backyard.

I was going to the company today, but after what happened, I am not leaving the house right now. It's too dangerous.

But tomorrow I have the circle meeting and I have to be there. I already missed last week's, and there are certain things we have to discuss concerning Jeremy Stone. He was responsible for some 'shipments' and now we have to see who will take some of his work.

I can take some and get some help from my friends in the mafia, but again, I have to focus on my personal life right now. I might die any minute.

"No, I am fine." He replies as he walks with me.

"As you wish." I say and sit on the chair. He takes the seat in front of me.

"You are okay right?" He asks worriedly.

"I am, you?" I ask as I check his face and body for any injury.

I have already done that of course, but just to make sure I did it again.

"Yes, I am." He nods.

Awkward silence...

What should I say?

I hear some footsteps and look to my left to see Donte and Gino coming towards us.

"Ma'am." Donte nods.

"What is it?" I ask them.

"We just came to tell you that we maximized the security. We recruited 20 new bodyguards to protect the mansion, as well as, you." Gino replies as he looks at my neck again.

Can't he take the hint?

That I don't want to talk to him?

I sent him a glare, but he still didn't look away.

"Come with me." I order Gino and walk farther.

Alessandro looked confused and was about to come with me when I stopped him with my hand.

Gino and I walk and we stop just a little bit farther than Donte and Alessandro.

"Who are you?" I ask firmly.

Just so you don't get lost, when I first met Gino, he said something about the scar on my neck. I didn't really pay that much attention to it, but yesterday night, I thought about it.

Gino clearly knows me from somewhere, and I clearly know him. I couldn't pinpoint as to where I met him, but I'll never forget those green eyes. I know them from somewhere.

"I am heart-broken that you don't remember me." He replies fake-sadly.

"I know we know each other, but from where?"

"Does Andre Valentino rings a bell?" He asks with a smirk as he opens his arms waiting for me to hug him.

Andre Valentino...Andre Valentino...Andre Va-

FUCK

"Gino Valentino? My long lost cousin Gino Valentino?" I shrieked.

"In the flesh!" He replies and I jump into his arms.

Trust me, I have never done that before, like ever. But I know this man...he is my brother figure. I remember when I was 14, he and his family suddenly disappeared. I still don't know why.

"Where have you been?" I ask, still couldn't believe my eyes.

"Here and there—didn't Annie tell you?"

"She knows?!"

"Well...I told here earlier this morning, but I guess she didn't tell you because of what happened." He explains.

"I can't believe I have family left." I look at him, mesmerized.

"I can't believe I finally found you! You disappeared after...you know."

"Yeah...I went to Britain for a bit to get away from everything."

"Well, I am glad I found you sis." He hugs me again, tighter this time.

Suddenly, someone clears their throat.

"Oh—Gino, this is my bodyguard Alessandro, Alessandro, this is Gino; my cousin." I introduce.

Don't know why I did that, but...yeah.

They shake hands, but Alessandro seems a bit...or actually so angry.

"I'll leave you guys now—see you later." Gino says and leaves.

"How come you just knew he's your cousin?" Alessandro asks as we walk back to the table.

"We haven't seen each other since I was fourteen—people change."

"I don't trust him."

"You don't have too."

"But you do?"

"I do."

"Well, you shouldn't Amalia—you don't know him."

"This conversation is over." I say and make my way inside, but a hand grabs my arm, pushing me back.

"I am sorry for...you know—yelling and all that. I haven't been on my best behavior."

"It's okay. Make sure it doesn't happen again."

"It won't." He nods. His hand is still on my arm.

A phone rings and Alessandro immediately answers.

"Hello baby." He smiles through the screen.

"Hi daddy!!!—" She giggles, "—I miss you."

"I miss you too darling—how have you been?"

"Annoiato." She huffs, "—I want to see you dad—and Amalia too."

Her confessions shocks me a little bit. I didn't think that she would ever think of me, or even misses me, and for some reason, I like that she is.

I walk up to Alessandro and peek through the screen to see her eyes widen and a smile covers her beautiful tiny lips.

"Amaliaaa!" She happily yells.

"Hello Lily, how are you?"

"I am good, I have missed you. I miss Gus too."

"Gus and I have missed you too—we cannot wait to see you." I smile as I look up at Alessandro to find him looking at me with a smile on his lips.

"Daddy pleaseee, come get me."

"You know I can't pumpkin, but we will see each other on the week-ends." He tries to convince her.

"But I want to be with you."

"I promise, I am working on it."

"LILY! Who are you talking to?" A voice yells.

"Bye daddy! Bye Amalia, I love you!"

And then, she hangs up.

He was about to say something, but I cut him off, "I will do whatever I can to help you get your daughter back. Whatever it takes."———

I whimper as I open my eyes.

Another nightmare.

I look to my right to see Gus cuddled up. I get closer to him and hug him tight. He is probably the only one who could make me feel safe and relaxed.

I close my eyes again to welcome sleep, but it never came. So, I decided to go to the backyard because I need an air.

Opening the door to my room, I walk slowly, making sure I don't make any noise. The room to my right is Annie's and to my left is Alessandro's. He stays here during the weekdays, and goes to his house on the weekends with his daughter.

I wonder if he will leave his job when he wins his daughter's cust ody...will he leave me?

I chuckle. Of course, he'll leave. They all do.

Sighing, I open the backdoor and step out. I breathe in, feeling relaxed immediately. There is something about smelling nature. It has this distinctive smell that makes you feel so refreshed and relaxed.

"Couldn't sleep?" A voice says from behind. I instantly knew who it was.

"No, you?"

"No—I heard your room door open, so I thought something was wrong." I smile at his confession. He was worried about me.

"Nothing happened, don't worry—you can go back to sleep Alessandro."

I hear his footsteps closer until I felt him beside me. I glance at him and found him looking to where I was looking earlier.

"The sky is beautiful, isn't it." He comments.

"It is."

I find myself looking at his face, taking in every feature. His beautiful ocean eyes, his disheveled blond hair, and his tiny pink lips, stirs something within me. What could it be Amalia?

"Isn't it funny?—I have been here what? Few days and we have already lived so many things."

I don't know how to engage in a conversation...why is he talking? I don't know what to say.

"Yeah...life works in a mysterious way." I reply hesitantly.

"I know this is none of my business, but uh...do you..I don't know like-"

"Are you alright kids?" A sleepy voice says.

Annie.

"Yeah, we are okay—are you?" I ask.

"I am. Just heard voices and panicked a little."

"Sorry about that." Alessandro replies.

"No problem—go to sleep, you have work tomorrow."

With that, she left, with us trailing behind her.

Before I enter my room, I turn towards him and ask, "what did you want to tell me?"

"Oh..it's nothing. We can talk tomorrow." He smiles and mumbled a goodnight.

"Alessandro!"

"Yes?"

"I am glad you're here."

"Glad am here too."

With that, each one of us entered their rooms and called it a day.

I cannot believe I told him that tho. I never opened up to anyone before and I never thought I will. I mean...I did open up once in my lifetime, but promised myself that I'll never do it again, especially not with a guy.

I just hope he doesn't turn out like the rest.

————

I hope you liked this chapter you guys!!!! Don't forget to vote, comment, and share! It really means a lot!

Also, what do you think happened to Amalia? Why does she not trust anyone? Especially men?

Word count: 2305

# 6. The Circle

Gino^^^

AMALIA

Red or black?

Red is more sexy, and black is more sophisticated and elegant.

I want to look a little intimidating, what should I choose?

Looking between the two dresses, I settled on Black. I want to look intimidating today, yet elegant. Today I am going to the weekly circle meeting, and I can't wait to see everyone's expression when they see me.

Of course, not everyone thinks I am dead, just the guilty ones, who sent those men after me.

Putting my hair up in a ponytail, I look over myself in the mirror, and feel satisfied with how I look.

Walking down the spiral stairs, I make my way to the dining room to eat my breakfast. I am 15 minutes late today, as I took my sweet time in the morning.

"Bongiorno." I greet Annie and Alessandro, "—where is Isabella?"

"She called sick today—I told her to stay at home." Annie explains as I clench my jaw.

Why didn't I know earlier? I have some work that needs to be done.

"Fine." I roll my eyes and sit on my usual seat, at the head of the table.

"Sorry for being late." I say and start eating, with them following me.

Today's breakfast: the typical Italian breakfast prima colazione, which consists of caffè latte (hot milk with coffee) with bread rolls and butter and jam.

I love it.

"Are you sure you want to go to the meeting today?" Annie asks worriedly.

"I have too. We have to discuss Jeremy's death and who's going to take after his work." I reply as I bite a piece of bread roll.

"Isn't it dangerous?"

"It is, but I don't care—besides, Alessandro and Gino will be with me." I explain earning a frown from Alessandro.

"Gino? Why is he coming? I thought you need one only." Alessandro asks, clearly annoyed.

I send him a glare and don't reply to him.

"Annie, stay home and don't go out. Donte will be with you and the rest of the guards."

"Okay, don't worry about me—worry about yourself now."

"I can do both." I say as I drink up my latte.

As we finish breakfast, Gino comes into the dining room.

Some part of me doesn't trust him fully, but we'll see.

"Morning beautiful." He says as he places his arm around my shoulder.

I quickly slap his arm away.

"Don't touch me." I roll my eyes playfully, but with a serious tone.

"Ouch." He says, putting his palm on his heart, acting as if he's hurt.

I felt a pair of eyes glaring at the side of my head, but I ignored it knowing very well that it's Alessandro. I just don't know what's going on with him.

Bipolar.

"What time are we leaving?" He asks as he takes one bread roll from my plate.

He used to always do that when we were younger.

"Now." I say as I stand up and Alessandro doing the same.

We walk out of the dining room, but not before giving Annie a kiss.

It's weird that sometimes I call her by her name, and other times I call her mamma.

Well...it's not weird but still.

Gino was about to open the door for me, but Alessandro beats him to it.

"Thanks." I say and step inside.

"Damn...you look really intimidating." Gino chuckles as he looks at me from head to toe.

"That's the point." I casually reply.

Gino is sitting right across of me, while Alessandro is sitting beside me. A little bit closer than he usually does.

I glance at him, his face is a dark shade of red, as if he had a fight few minutes ago.

I turn around and look outside the window, at the trees passing by. My mind goes to Gino for some reason, and questions swirl inside my head.

How did he find me? Why is he here? Why is he working for me and didn't tell me who he is when he first came? What had he been doing before? Why did he ask about my scar the first time I saw him, acting as if he didn't know me then?

And finally, is he here to kill me?

Now...I know you might say that he is my cousin and I should trust him since I know him, BUT I haven't seen him in eleven years, a lot could have happened.

I glance at him and find him scrolling through his phone. I try to look into his phone to find him playing a game.

I am confused.

I don't think he's here to kill me...

The car suddenly stops, indicating that we arrived to our destination.

Stepping out of the car, I walk inside the building with Gino and Alessandro by each side. They are so close to me, afraid something might happen. I hope not.

We step into the elevator, pressing the 12th floor. We are the only ones here.

I am standing a little close to Alessandro and I could smell his cologne...god. It's intoxicating. I would smell it for the rest of my life, and I wouldn't get bored from it.

The elevator opens and we step out.

"Welcome back Ms. Ferrari." The main secretary greeted. I just nodded.

When I come to this building, my attitude changes and I become someone else. Someone who no one tolerates.

Opening the door to the meeting room, I see shocked faces. Few of them.

A smirk make its way to my lips as I look into each one of their eyes.

"Ladies—" I greeted the ladies, "—and gentlemen." I nod.

"Hello Amalia, we missed you last week." One of the members; Collin Dark, says.

"Yeah, I was busy." I casually say as I sit on my usual seat, which is at the head of the time.

Why? Because I like to, and when I like something, I do anything to get it.

Plus, they cannot defy me, which is why they do things behind my back.

"Now, let's talk about Jeremy." I start off saying, "—as you all know, he died few days ago—actually he was murdered, and now there is no one from his family to do his work. He doesn't have sons and his daughter is still young."

"There are three jobs that he used to do and they were, drug shipments, car supply shipments, and weapons shipments—now, who can take what?" I conclude as I look at each on of them.

"I can take the car supply shipments. I know someone who can help me with that—plus, I have always wanted to do this type of work." Clair Carter says.

She wanted his work a long time ago? She could be a suspect. Maybe she killed him?

But no, he was killed for one reason only and that's the thing he wanted to tell me, but failed to do so.

But she could be one of the killers. I am sure it's not only one.

"I can take drug shipments." Joseph Cintino offers.

No one else says anything about the weapon shipments, so I decide to speak up.

"Fine—I'll take the weapons shipments."

"So, how's everything going?" I ask.

"My hotels and Casinos are good. This year is good for us." Joseph says, "—and I am sure the drug shipments will make us benefit more."

I just nod.

"My car company is doing well." Clair says casually.

The rest of the members talked about their work and how they are doing. I didn't talk about mine because I don't really like to share that kind of information to them. I don't trust them.

"By the way Joseph, I am coming to one of your clubs tomorrow, reserve a VIP room for me."

"Which club?"

"I'll text you." I say as I stand up.

I didn't want to say which club in front of them all because I have to be careful. Besides, Joseph is a sweetheart he won't tell anyone. But still, I don't trust him.

Sweet guys like him tend to turn out the worst.

I make my way out with my bodyguard following behind me.

"Ms, Ferrari!" The secretary; Josette, calls.

"Yes?"

"I really like your outfit."

"Thanks." I roll my eyes and step into the elevator.

"That's kinda rude." Gino remarks.

"Good, because I am rude." I reply as I press the ground floor.

He just chuckles.

I turn to look at Alessandro to find him looking straight, his jaw clenched, and his fingers tapping on his other hand.

He is awfully quiet, and I don't like it.

"Gino, I would like you to go home and stay with Annie." I say, grabbing Alessandro's attention.

"But I can't leave you alone!" He argues.

I was about to reply when Alessandro cut me off by saying, "she's not alone, I am with her."

Gino rolls his eyes and looks at me again. "Are you sure?"

"Yes, I am." I say and he leaves.

"So, are we walking?" Alessandro asks.

"Yes, we are."

——

We arrive at a small, cozy café. We take a seat and I say what I have been waiting to say since morning.

"So, what wrong with you?"

"Me? Nothing. Why would you ask that?" He replies, clearly lying.

"Don't lie to me, spit it out, Alessandro."

"There is nothing to spit out but my saliva." He jokes, but I don't laugh.

Not because it's not funny, but because I want the real reason.

"That was funny!" He chuckles.

"No, no it wasn't—now answer."

"Fine, I don't like him. I don't trust him. I hate him. Why is he even here? He's acting weird as if he knows you since childhood." He starts to ramble.

"Technically, I do know him from childhood, he is my cousin, remember?"

"I know that, but I don't trust him Amalia, and I don't want you to be around him." He finalizes, shocking me to the core.

Why is he acting like this?

"Remember that you are my employee Alessandro, and I am the one who can change your life or turn it upside down." I firmly say.

I always manipulate people and I always enjoy it, but with him, I didn't like it one bit.

"Is that so?" He scoffs, "—fine Ms, Ferrari, I apologize for my lack of respect. It won't happen again."

What the hell.

Stop calling me that!

"Good."

We went back home and he didn't once talk to me. Why is he acting this way?

A question that I won't seem to know.

"Follow me to my office." I instruct Alessandro.

"Yes, Ms. Ferrari?" He says as he closes the door.

"Stop calling me that." I spat angrily. He's getting on my nerves.

Big time.

"Well, you are my boss, aren't you?"

"Yes, I am, and I am telling you to stop calling me that!"

"Why!?" He yells.

It just dawned to me that his face is centimeters away.

"I don't want you calling me that! It's Amalia to you!" I reply.

Suddenly, his hands circle my waist, holding me tight. His breathing became hard as if he's so so angry. I look up into his eyes, and see many emotions swirl inside of them.

Anger, passion, lust, hunger...so many other emotions that I could not pinpoint.

What is happening?

What is he doing?

His face leans down and I panic.

He wants to kiss me. He clearly wants to kiss me. I can't do that! We can't do that.

"We can't do that." I voice my thoughts as I step back, leaving him cold.

He blinks and realization hits him.

"I..I am sorry—I shouldn't have tried anything." He clears his throat.

"It's fine—make sure it doesn't happen again." I say and he nods.

"What did you want to talk about?"

"Oh...I just want to ask you about Lily, but it's okay, we can talk tomorrow." I quickly say as I couldn't control the intense beating of my heart. I feel like my heart is going to explode any minute.

"Okay, good night."

"Good night."

——

I make my way to the backyard to find Gino sitting with Donte. Why are they still here?

"Why are you still here?" I ask.

"I just wanted to wait till you come back, to make sure you're safe."

"Donte, you can leave." I order him and he gets up and leaves.

"We need to talk."

"What is it?"

"Why are you here Gino? After all those years? Why now?"

He looks taken aback as he nervously starts to fidget with his fingers.

He's hiding something.

"Do not lie to me Gino, I know you are hiding something."

"The reason we disappeared ten years ago, is because my mother was murdered by one of my father's enemies. We had to move away to hide, so we went to America for few years. When I turned 20, I discovered that my father and brother, worked with some mafia.

They tried to force me to join them, but I didn't want to, so I ran away. I later traveled to London because that's the only place they wouldn't think to search in. I stayed there and worked to gain some money. I then came here and looked for you and your family. I didn't know they died when I left Amalia, I am sorry."

Even though I asked him one specific question, he told me the story of his life.

You might call me heartless, but I don't care.

"I repeat, why are you here, Gino."

"Because I think I know who killed your parents, and I am here to help you take them down."

——

I hope you liked this chapter guys!!!! What do you think?

Who do you think killed Amalia's parents? And why?

Don't forget to vote and comment!!'

Xoxo,

Word count: 2320

# 7. Gino the Sus

Sorry for the late chapter and I hope you enjoy Amalia's and Alessandro's moments :)

AMALIA

Always listen to your gut, even if it tells you that your mother is a bad person, or father for that matter.

I have always listened to it and here I am, getting fooled by my supposed cousin--at least that's what he thought.

My gut never failed me and it is not going to right now.

"Who is it?" I ask, looking straight into his eyes to see if he's lying. He isn't.

"I am not exactly sure, but I think the Russian mafia killed your parents. Your father was in debt, and he stumbled upon Joseph Lebedev; the Russian mob, and asked for some money to pay his debts--when he couldn't pay back...well, he killed them." He explains nervously.

Before anything else, let's analyze. First, he says that he is and I quote, "I am not exactly sure," and that immediately tells me that he is lying because after that, he clearly tells me the entire story, as if he knows it. As if he...

No, it can't be.

"When did you find out?"

"3 years ago."

"You waited 3 years to tell me?"

"I told you, I couldn't find you."

He couldn't find me, yet...he knew I lived in Italy, how?

"I believe you." I lie smoothly.

It is time that things change. I cannot work alone and I clearly need some assistance, and there is only one family that could help me with this stupid guy.

"Thank you." He smiles warmly and gives me a hug that I despised a lot.

"We better go to sleep." I announce as I stand up, breaking our hug.

"By the way Amalia, don't tell anyone. It is dangerous." He warns seriously.

"Of course, I am not stupid." I smile and walk inside the house.

Walking up the spiral stairs, I make my way to Alessandro's room. I wanted to wait for tomorrow, but I have to speak with him now.

Knocking on his door, I proceed and open it to find Alessandro sleeping. I quietly close it behind me and walk towards him. I am about to stretch my hand to wake him up, when suddenly I am flipped and my back hits the bed, with my arms above my head.

"Fuck! Amalia, what are you doing here? I thought you were an intruder." He groans as he gets off me, and stretches his hand to pick me up.

I take it gladly, even though I preferred our previous position.

"Lower your voice!" I hiss, "—we have to talk."

"Couldn't it wait for tomorrow?" He whispers.

"No, it's important."

He motions his hand towards the bed telling me to sit, and I did. His room smells like him. Of course, it does! it's his room...god.

I just notice that he is shirtless too. Shit.

"Umm." I clear my throat, looking everywhere but him.

"So?"

"Well...I mean--could you put a shirt on?" I snap as I feel my cheeks burn with embarrassment. Couldn't I just control myself?

A smirk makes its way onto his lips as he stands up to grab a shirt from the closet.

"This good?" He points at his body and I nod.

I suddenly regret telling him to wear a shirt, but...I had to.

"Okay, so I was talking with Gino and you were right."

"Right about what exactly?"

"Everything."

"What everything?" He frowns.

God! is he stupid or what?

"Everything Aless! about not trusting him and he might not be a good person, and all that." I whisper-yell.

Wait...Aless?

"Aless, ha." He bites his bottom lip as I lose my breath for few seconds. What have I done?

"Focus."

"Well, I know I am right, I always am."

"Cocky much?" I say as he smiles a genuine smile. That made me smile too.

"What did he say?" He asks as his playfulness drifted away, and a serious look replaced it.

"Nothing important." I try to ignore the subject. I cannot tell him about my past...not now at least.

"It is obviously important because if it weren't, you wouldn't suspect him." He replies.

"I didn't even trust him that much!" I shriek, but quickly cover my mouth as I don't want anyone to hear.

"Yeah, not at all. If you didn't suspect him now, you would have kissed him tomorrow." He rolls his eyes, getting annoyed by the second.

Is he jealous? because he looks like it.

"Yeah, you're right. I would've have." I say as a smirk made its way to my lips. He turns towards me and a frown covered his face.

"I was only joking." He says, still frowning.

"I wasn't." I bite my bottom lip and stand up, ready to leave.

"Are you leaving?"

"Yeah, why? you want me to sleep here with you?"

"What? No, I-I didn't mean that." He replies nervously, scratching the back of his neck.

"Good night."

"Good night, Amalia."

———

This is really a torture for us girls. I mean...it is really hard to choose an outfit. How do you do it?

Looking back and forth between my formal suits, I frown because I can't decide which one to wear. I have an important meeting today, and I want to look my absolute best.

"Honey, are you ready? Alessandro and Isabella are waiting for you downstairs." Annie says as she enters my room.

Isabella and Alessandro together? again?

"I can't decided which one to choose."

"Choose the white one, it is beautiful—actually, everything is beautiful on you." She hugs me from the side.

"Grazie, mamma."

I pick out the white formal suit, and walk to my walk-in closet to change. When I finish, I style my hair, putting it up in a ponytail; a firm one. I apply a little bit of makeup, my usual makeup routine.

Walking downstairs, I receive my tea and step into the living room.

There they are, talking and laughing like last time. I clear my throat, grabbing their attention immediately.

"Good morning, Ms. Ferrari." Isabella professionally, yet enthusiastically greets.

"Good morning." I nod to them both.

"Ms. Ferrari, here's a report of everything happened at the company the last few days." Isabella says, handing my a red file.

I open it and scan through it quickly. Our sales got higher by 15%, which is extremely good. We got many new clients, who are eager to work with us, and that's good.

"Good job, Isabella." I give her the file back.

"Are you coming today to the company?" She asks hesitantly.

"No, I have a meeting outside with a special client, so I won't be coming today—You handle everything."

"Okay." She nods and leaves.

"Where are we going today?" Alessandro asks as he takes a seat beside me, a little bit closer than he should as usual.

"We are going to visit a friend of mine, who will help me with the issue I told you about yesterday in your room."

"You were in his room?" A voice asks and I wince as I forgot Annie was still here.

"For work." I correct myself. She nods and leaves, but not before sending me a wink.

God...this woman.

"Why was she surprised that you were in my room?" Alessandro's voice is so close and I could feel his breath on my neck.

"That's...none of your business." I hesitate a little bit.

"Tell me Amalia.." he groans.

"I just..you know...haven't socialized a lot with men, and now hearing that I was in your room...she thought.." I tried to sound firm, but I couldn't.

"So, I am lucky then." He says, making my heart beat faster.

I clear my throat and say firmly as I move away from him, "We have to leave. It will take us almost 13h to arrive."

"Where is it?" He frowned.

"Florence."

"Are we going to spend the night there?"

"Probably."

———I am so bored. 13 hours in a plane is just torture. I look to my side to find Alessandro sleeping. Of course, he's sleeping.

"Alessandro..." I place my palm on his cheek, trying to wake him up.

I should leave him alone and let him sleep, but I am bored.

"Alessandro." I call again, but his eyes are still shut close.

An idea comes to my mind and I smirk at what's going to happen next. I unfasten my seatbelt and lean in onto his face. I smile and take out my tongue, gliding it on his cheek. He immediately jerks up, looking confused.

I just laugh.

"Did you just...lick me?" He asks, a bit flustered.

"You wouldn't wake up, so I thought that would work."

"Did we arrive?"

"Not yet."

"Then why did you wake me up?" He shrieks.

"Watch it." I warn, but a smile made its way to my lips.

For some odd reason, I couldn't be a bitch to him anymore.

"What do you want then." He rolls his eyes as he looks around, probably looking for Gino, who is sleeping in the bedroom.

Gino came with us because I cant trust him being alone at my house, especially when Annie and Gus are there.

"I am bored." I pout playfully.

I cannot believe I am acting like this with him. I don't like it.

He takes me aback when he leans in, grabbing my waist in the process, "what do you want me to do?"

What the fuck are you doing!

That's what I wanted to tell him, but I kept my mouth shut. I couldn't move.

I could feel his breath on my neck as he looked to be smelling my hair. Thank god I showered today.

"Alessandro..." I tried to form a question, but came up with nothing but his name.

"Mmm?"

His fingertips start going in circles around my waist, making my heart beat ten times faster.

As if on cue, we hear a voice from behind and he immediately backs away.

"Did we arrive yet?" Gino asks as he rubs his eyes.

"One hour left." I reply firmly.

Thank god I regained control of myself.

"By the way, who are we meeting again?" Gino asks curiously.

"You'll see." I smile and look out of the window.

"By the way Amalia, can we talk? Just the two of us." Gino says, looking at Alessandro as he said the last part.

"Whatever you want to say, you can say it here." I reply meanly.

Bitch mode back on

"Umm, fine then—about what I said yesterday, are we going to do something about it? Is this meeting for that thing?"

"Who knows, maybe. I am the boss here, remember?" I reply coldly earning a confused look from Gino, and a satisfied look from Alessandro.

The pilot announces that we finally landed, and we unfasten our seatbelts.

As we walk down the stadium, I clutch Alessandro's arm as I was about to fall from the heavy wind.

He grabs my waist, steading my tightly, as we walk to the car.

"Thank you." I murmur and he nods.

I give the driver the address and we drive off.

As we are on our way, I think about everything that happened today. I don't know what's happening between me and Alessandro, but it is definitely something scary, and I don't like it. We are too close and comfortable with each other.

But...I still kinda like it.

"Are we sure we are going to the right place? It looks like we are driving into a forest." Gino comments as he looks around.

"No, we are on the right track." I smirk as I see his face pale.

Does he know where we are going?

——

I hope you liked this chapter guys!!!!!

Where do you think they are going? And why did Gino sound so afraid?

I am so sorry that this chapter is not as long as the other, but I am trying to update frequently.

Thanks for reading

Word count: 2013.

# 8. A Meeting With My Allies

AMALIA

"Welcome to our home!" Leila González greets, opening her arms for me to hug, and I do.

"Thank you, Leila."

"Nice to see you again, Amalia." Demetrio; Leila's husband, greets, giving me a brotherly hug.

"It's nice to see you too." I smile, "—these are Alessandro and Gino." I point at the gentlemen.

Demetrio nods and motions for us to follow him.

Their mansion is quite beautiful. It's a three-story mansion, with a huge garden in the front. As I walk, I look around in awe. I have always knew that Demetrio and Leila have good taste in decorating houses. I mean...when I travelled to the U.S, I visited their home in a small town called Galena, and it was quite beautiful.

We stroll inside the house, following Demetrio to what seems to be the living room. Leila left to the kitchen, probably to get us something.

"So, to what I owe this pleasure." He smiles as he sits down.

I glance at Gino and Alessandro, and nod my head conveying the message that I want them to wait outside.

After they left, I turn my attention back to Demetrio.

"I have two propositions." I start as he sits up to listen, "—first, I would like you to help me with some shipments—you know, from one country to the other. Second, I want you to hold someone hostage and learn everything about him, I believe he is behind my parent's death."

His eyes widened at the mention of my parent's death.

"What kind of shipments?" He firstly asks.

"Weapons." I reply earning a nod in approval.

"And who is the man?"

"Gino—the one who is standing outside." As soon as I say that, he stands up looking angry and pissed.

"And you brought him to my house?" He growls.

"Well, I figured you'd say yes, so I brought him with me."

He takes out his phone and calls someone to come. After few minutes, an unfamiliar man appeared in the living room.

"Yes, Demetrio?"

"River, I want you to take care of something." Demetrio orders earning a huff from River.

"But, I have a date with Mia." He groans.

"Can't you leave my daughter for a minute and listen to your boss?"

"Fine." He rolls his eyes and leaves, but halts as he turns back towards us.

"Who is the guy?"

How did he know that Demetrio wants him to take care of a guy?

"He is the one standing outside—not the handsome one, the other." I reply this time with a smirk.

He nods and leaves.

"I didn't know River is dating your daughter." I smirk as I see irritation covers his face.

"They are engaged—" he rolls his eyes, "—I don't like it." He huffs.

Demetrio González hates one thing in this world and that's, his daughter having a boyfriend.

No one and I mean no one should touch, glance, hurt, or any form of anything. In his thick skull, his daughter is his princess and will always be with him. He loves her that much.

He is over protective too.

"I mean...she's happy, right? That's what's important." I try to make him like the idea of her having a boyfriend a little, but I know it won't work.

"I guess, but still." He huffs again making me chuckle.

"He's in the basement." River's robotic voice announced.

"Good, thanks River, you can go back to your date." I smirk earning another huff from Demetrio.

"Why does he have to be with her 24/7?" He asks, groaning.

"That's what lover so. They stay together 24/7—weren't you glued to Leila when you fell in love with her?"

"Yes, I was." He smiles at the memory, making me smirk for the millionth time.

His smile quickly fades away, "but still."

I just roll my eyes. What could you say to a man who has a brain like his? Nothing.

"Lunch is ready!" Leila announces as she enters the living room.

"Thanks Leila, you didn't have to." I smile.

"Don't say that." She frowns.

"By the way, may I invite Alessandro to eat with us?"

"Of course!" Demetrio replies.

I make my way outside, but not before sending them a grateful smile.

I open the door to find Alessandro pacing back and forth, talking on the phone with his daughter.

"Okay, I gotta go baby, talk to you later, okay?"

"Okay, daddy! Kiss Amalia for me." Her beautiful voice says.

My cheeks are probably red now because of what she said. Kiss her for me? I have to ask him for the kiss then.

"Are we leaving?" Alessandro cut my thoughts off.

"No, we are going to eat lunch and then leave—come." I reply as I walk inside with him following me.

I sit across from Leila and Demetrio, with Alessandro beside me.

"Alessandro, isn't it?" Demetrio asks as he receives a nod from my handsome bodyguard.

"You must be very special to Amalia for her to invite you to lunch." He comments as my cheeks burn.

What the hell Demetrio!

"I guess so." Aless says as he looks at me.

"It's not that." I frown, "—it's that I have to trust him. Obligated." I explain, but none of them seem convinced, even Alessandro.

"Whatever you say." Leila smirks as she digs into the food.

"So, Amalia, you didn't tell me why you hired a personal bodyguard." Leila asks.

"I have a target on my back." I reply as I sip my orange juice.

"Oh god..."

"Who is it?" This time it's Demetrio.

"Not sure yet, but I think Gino is somehow involved."

"I told you he shouldn't be trusted." Alessandro grunts.

"You were just jealous, Alessandro." My honesty was flying out of my mouth.

"Jealous?—" he chuckles, "—why would I be jealous? He is not even near beautiful—he's clingy—extremely fake—and a liar." He starts to point out every thing in his list of 'why would I be jealous of Gino.'

"You clearly were jealous since you practically yelled at your boss." I remark, I turn my body towards his, and he did the same.

"I was doing that because I am your bodyguard, and I should warn you at times like these." He explains.

"You are—"

"Are you guys done?" Demetrio cuts me off as I glance at him to see him smirking.

Shit.

I forgot about them.

I clear my throat.

"We were just...you know." I say as I take a sip from my juice again. What could I have said, ha?

"Are you both sure you are not dating?" Leila smirks, making me and Alessandro choke.

"Yes!" We say in unison.

Of course, we are not dating.

I glare at Leila and she shuts up immediately.

"Hello!" Oh thank god.

I turn around and Mia is standing with River to her side.

"You two haven't left?" Leila asks.

"No, we are leaving now."

"What were you two doing?" Demetrio narrows his eyes, sending daggers to River.

"We were...umm—"

"God, Demetrio, it's none of your business, they are old enough to do whatever they want." I say as a smirk make its way to my red lips.

"No, absolutely not! Not whatever they want." He shrieks making us all laugh.

"How are you Amalia?" Mia asks.

"I am good sweetie, and you?"

"Good."

After lunch, Alessandro and I went back to the hotel

"You should have seen Gino's face when he was dragged by that boy." He chuckles.

"I am sure you were extremely satisfied and happy with the scene." I tease.

"Of course, I was. No more Gino." He sighs in relief as if Gino had been sitting on him for a while.

We reach our suite that thankfully has two rooms. We walk inside and place our luggage.

"This place is amazing." He compliments as he looks around.

"I always stay here when I come to Florence."

"You come here a lot?"

"No, only when I want to see Demetrio."

We go on our separate ways as each one of us go to their room.

I need a shower, a very long ass shower.

I enter the bathroom and close the door behind me. I unzip my dress, putting it aside, and step into the shower. The warm water rolls down my cold one, and I sigh.

This is so relaxing.

I clean my hear with the hotel's shampoo; something I despise a lot, and wash it off. I then scrub my body, removing any dirt.

I wrap a towel around my body and walk outside of the bathroom, into my room.

I pick out a silky red nightwear with its robe, and wear them.

I didn't forget the panties, don't worry.

I brush my long, brown hair, and apply a moisturizer on my face and body.

A sudden knock halts my moving hands, as my heart starts beating fast. Why? Who knows.

"Yes?"

"Are you done?"

"Yes."

The door opens revealing a breathtaking adonis. I rake my eyes along his body, taking in every inch.

He does the same.

He suck in his breath as his eyes shamelessly rake down my figure.

"I-I....I just wanted to know of you want to eat anything." He stutters, but quickly regained his focus.

"Sure." I swallow hard.

He nods and closes the door behind him.

After I finish everything, I walk out of my room. I see Alessandro sitting around the round table, waiting for me to come.

The food looks delicious from here. The smell fills my nostrils, and my mouth water.

I sit across from Aless, and we both dig into the food.

"I happened to have listened to your conversation with Lily." I start, getting his attention.

"She said something about me." I say as his eyes widen.

"Oh that." He coughs and I nod.

"She was just... you know, as a gesture of saying hello."

"Oh really? Because I wanted that kiss so bad." I look at my plate as I say this.

A part of me loves to tease, to make him blush, and to make him feel the same way I feel.

But what am I feeling?

Suddenly, he stands up and walks to me, dragging his chair along with him.

He sits and faces me.

"Where do you want it?" He asks innocently.

I swallow hard.

Why am I not powerful now?

Why am I doing this?

I said I didn't want to do it, yet here I am.

I am vulnerable and I hate it.

What if he turns out like that bastard?

No, he would never.

"Amalia?" He asks, worry covers his beautiful face.

"Ahh, sorry, my mind went somewhere." I nervously say as I drink my water.

"And to answer your question, I want it here." I say, pointing at my neck.

As much as I want it on my lips...but.

He leans in, grabbing my waist in the process. His firm hand grips protectively around my waist as if I will disappear.

I lean my head to the left, giving him more space.

His lips slowly but shortly, touch my neck, leaving not only one kiss but three. Three kisses.

He leans back and looks into my eyes. I am hypnotized.

"If I am not mistaken, Lily said a kiss, which means one." I innocently say.

He grabs my waist again, pushing me towards him, our chests touching, and I could feel his breath on my ear.

"The other two are just a brief of what I am going to do to you in the near future."

He says that and leaves to his room.

If you are asking what I am doing right now, I am just sitting, mouth agape, looking at his back as he disappears to his room.

For a moment, I couldn't breathe.

I regain my posture and make my way to my room.

———

"Finally! You're back." Annie exclaims as she extend her arms, giving me a hug.

"I miss you mamma."

"Miss you too baby."

"How was everything?" I ask as I look around the house.

"Nothing much, just Gus running around the house looking for you."

As if on cue, Gus strolls down the stairs, barking.

"Hey baby." I kneel and hug him.

"I miss you too." I giggle.

"You seem happy." Annie smirks, looking between my and Alessandro.

"Business went well." I quickly say.

She hums in response.

Alessandro and I walk up the stairs to go to our rooms.

My mind wonders to Gino. I hope Demetrio gets something out of him. I already told Demetrio everything about the situation. How Gino might be related to my parent's death, everything.

Suddenly, I am pushed back, my back hitting my bedroom door.

"Alessandro? What are you doing?"

"I cannot take it anymore." He groans and slams his lips onto mine.

———

Hey guys! I hope you liked this chapter I had so much fun writing it.

What do you think of what happened?

Also, for those of you who read Mia González, did you think that Amalia was going to meet them or not?

Don't forget to vote, comment, and share!!!

Thank you

Word count: 2202

# 9. Some of The Past

AMALIA

Looking into his beautiful brown eyes, we keep staring at each other, not knowing what to do, or more specifically, what we did.

We just kissed. A passionate kiss.

I liked it and he did as well.

But.

There will always be a but.

I push him back a little, creating a small space between us. Thoughts swarm in my head as I could not wrap my head on what just happened.

Thoughts of my ex came back and I just...I don't like what I am feeling.

I know that Alessandro is nothing like my ex, but I used to say that about him too.

He was amazing.

What if Alessandro's the same?

But no...he couldn't be. He's an angel.

My breathing increases as I think about what happened to me because of that bastard, and suddenly, I couldn't breathe.

"Amalia? Are you okay?" He worriedly asks, putting his right hand on my left shoulder.

I motion with my left hand, signaling that I cannot talk, and I start walking outside of my room, making my way into Annie's.

She's the only person who could help me when I get a panic attack.

Opening the door into her room, she jolts up from her sleep, probably thinking an intruder.

"Amalia? What's going on?" She runs to me and hugs me.

I couldn't speak and she understood that.

Sitting in her arms, she sings and plays with a strand of my hair. This thing really helps me calm down.

"What happened, baby?" She asks softly.

"Thoughts of that day came back." I simply say.

"But why? Nothing could trigger that unless something happened. What happened?"

"Nothing important, mamma."

"Tell me."

I roll my eyes at her attitude because I know that she would stay up till the morning asking me if I didn't tell her.

"Alessandro and I...kissed."

She doesn't say anything for few seconds, but later graces me with her beautiful voice.

"Finally, I could feel the sexual tension between you too—" her happy voice irritated me, "—but still, it must've triggered that incident." He completes sadly.

"I should stay away from him."

"No! You shouldn't."

"I should. I should stay alone for the rest of my life. You remember what happened with Castelo?—she couldn't bear me. Alessandro will be the same."

"How do you know that? Do not judge before you know for sure."

"Mamma, I am a narcissistic bitch, a manipulator, a sadistic person. Not to mention, broken too.

I flinch from everything, even a touch. How do you think Alessandro will react to all of this when he knows the real me?"

"Alessandro is different—besides, when he's beside you, you do not flinch. You are comfortable with him." She explains, trying to change my mind.

"What if he gets disgusted with me because of my past?" My voice cracks.

"You cannot know until you find out, but what I know is that Alessandro is a good man."

Few years ago, I was in relationship with a man called Castelo. He was my everything. I didn't see anything other than him. He was my entire life. I loved him so much that I gave him my virginity. I was so sure that he is the man for me, and that I will marry him one day, but everything changed when he accused me of cheating.

I was very weak, quiet, and a person who doesn't say anything when someone yells at me or anything. I used to accept whatever he used to tell me because I loved him. I loved him more than I did for myself, but I wasn't naïve.

That day, I came back home; one we shared, and found him waiting for me in the living room.

I came in late because my boss at that time had requested for me to stay and work on some stuff, nothing more nothing less.

How did Castelo manage to accuse me of cheating with my boss? I don't know, and I still don't know how he found out, not that I really did.

That day was the worst day of my life. Of course, not worse than my parent's death, but from that day, everything changed. I changed. I changed into this person I am today. Maybe, I should give some credits to him for turning me to the person I am today, but again, I miss my old self. I miss being and feeling safe. I miss kindness, and for some reason, I cannot go back to my old self.

I was beaten and nearly died. I still don't know how I survived.

After I recovered, which actually took 5 whole months, I searched for him, and when I found him, I killed him.

And that's when I met Demetrio González and Leila.

They helped me with everything, and gave me a portion of money, so that Annie and I could start fresh since I was fired from my job for being absent for 5 months.

No one knew about what happened to me because I killed a man, and no one was supposed to know. That's what Demetrio told me.

Since that day, Demetrio and I became good friends.

I walk out of Annie's room, and make my way to mine. Thank god, Alessandro probably went to his room. He didn't follow me to Annie's room.

I put my head on the pillow and take a deep breath. After few minutes, Gus joins me, and cuddles with me.

Tomorrow is a new day, and tomorrow, I have to get back to my old self. Ever since Alessandro came into my life, I haven't been the same, and I do not like it. I was never this emotional. I am a bad person, I killed.

He deserves someone better than me.

~ ~ ~ ~ ~ ~ ~ ~ ~

"You are so funny!" A voice giggles.

I walk into the living room to find Isabella laughing and giggling like always. Giggling to what Alessandro said.

"Good morning, Ms. Ferrari!" Isabella greets enthusiastically.

I look at her and roll me eyes; something her and Alessandro noticed.

I sit on the chair, putting my leg on top of the other, and sipping from the tea Annie gave me when I first came downstairs.

The look on my face screams anger, and I make sure everyone sees it. I am so mad to the point that I want to fire Isabella right here, right now...along with Alessandro.

"Isabella, I want you to meet with Jordan Park at the Lagoona Hotel at 3P.M." I start as I put my tea on the table. "He will share some ideas of our partnership on a project. Tell me what you think about them, but do not accept nor reject."

"Okay, ma'am." She nods and leaves.

Alessandro glances my way, but I pay no attention to him. Today is called, "Ignoring Alessandro day."

"Did Demetrio call?" I ask Annie.

"No, he didn't. I think it is going to take a while till Gino confesses anything."

Mhmm...

Suddenly, the doorbell rings. I see Ashelia hurries to open the door. I hear faint voices, but I could not make out who it is.

After a minute or so, Ashelia walks in with someone. I look up and the tea cup slides out of my hand, onto the floor, upon seeing her.

Great.

"Amalia..." Her timid but once sassy voice says.

I glance at Annie, a horrid expression covers her face as she looks at my dear sister. I glance at Alessandro and confusion covers his face.

I, on the other hand, have a smirk on. Why? because of what I am going to do next.

"Rebecca." I fake smile, "What are you doing here?" I ask as I look at her outfit. So ugly.

Karma indeed did her good.

"Can we talk? Alone?" She says nervously. Where did her arrogant ass go?

"Whatever you want to say, say it here, sister." I smirk, knowing that she needs my help, probably with money.

"Amalia...pleas-"

"Say it here!" I yell this time, shocking everyone. Alessandro the most.

I stand up and make my way to hers.

"You shouldn't have come here." I say dangerously as I see a tear rolls down onto her cheek.

"Please, Amalia...I am so sorry." She pleads, looking everywhere but at me.

I do what I have been dreaming of doing for a long time. I know it is not a good thing to do, but I want to do it. I might look like a crazy person, or even merciless, but I do it nevertheless.

I take her by her hair, dragging her behind me, as I walk to the front door. Her screams fill the living room, but I act oblivious.

Annie pleads to let her go, but I do no such thing.

When I reach the front door, I open it, and throw her out.

"I never want to see your face ever again, Rebecca, and if I did, I will kill you like I killed him." I say and close the door.

I feel so much better.

I turn around to find Annie and Alessandro standing, and looking at me with disapproved expression. That make me roll my eyes.

I do that a lot.

"You told her to come, didn't you?"

"You two have to talk!" Annie argues.

This is not the first time Annie does something like this. Two years ago, the same thing happened, but the difference was that I didn't take her by the hair. I don't know why even though I was angry at her, unlike now.

Right now, I do not care about her...at all.

"You don't tell me what to do, Annie." I harshly say.

"Yes, I DO! I AM YOUR MOTHER!"

"YOU ARE NOT!" That's what I wanted to say, but I didn't. I don't want to hurt her feelings.

"Yes, you are, but you have to respect what I want, and talking to her--" I point at the door, "--is not what I want."

"When are you going to let that go? She is your only family for god's sake! Stop being childish, GROW UP!" She yells in front of Alessandro. Everything that happened, happened in front of him.

"If you don't like how I am acting, then leave. Go live with that bitch." I say with no emotion, making my way out to the backyard.

It hurts me knowing that Annie is standing kind of in Rebecca's side. I know she doesn't mean to do that; she just wants us to get back together, but that's how she is making me feel.

No one ever chooses me...only me.

"Hey..." His soft, calm voice says. I close my eyes as I listen to his beautiful voice.

"If you are here to tell me how harsh I was on Annie, then leave." I harshly say.

As soon as I say that, he shakes his head, and walks towards me. Standing in front of me, he trace his fingers along my arm, making me shiver.

"I came to ask if you are okay." He gives me a weak smile that melts my insides.

"I am okay." I reply sharply.

"Look...I know you are not in the mood, but we have to talk abo ut...yesterday." He nervously says.

I don't know what to say. If I say that it is never going to happen again, then I will be a bitch; not that I am not.

If I say I liked it, then he will expect us to be together, and I can't do relationships now.

"Look, Alessandro, I liked it...the kiss, but it was just a kiss, nothing more." I say softly.

"I get it..." He nods and looks ahead, "I am sorry."

With that, he left.

~ ~ ~ ~ ~ ~

Hey guys!!!! I am extremely sorry for updating too late! but I was so busy and had a lot of things to do. I even considered to stop writing for some reason, but I am happy I didn't!

I hope you liked this chapter. I know a lot of bad things happened; annoying things, but don't worry! everything will come together.

What do you think of Amalia now? You learned her past and all, do you think she has the right to have this way?

Also, what do you think of Annie, now?

Rebecca is back...too.

Don't forget to vote, comment, and share!!!

Thanks & love you guys <3

Word Count: 2056

Instagram: the senoradenna

# 10. The Old Amalia is Back

CASSIE^^^—AMALIA

Stupido.

When she first came here, she was doing her work perfectly, that's until she started getting close with Alessandro. That's definitely the reason she started becoming lazy.

"Do it again." I harshly say, throwing the files her way.

"I am so sorry Ms. Ferrari, I'll do it again." Isabella replies, taking the files hesitantly from my desk, and turning around to leave.

But before she steps outside my office, I say, "I don't want you to apologize. I want results."

With that, she nodded and left.

I look around the office as my eyes glaring angrily at every corner of the room for no reason. It is as if they got me mad in the first place.

Today is Friday, which means that tomorrow is weekend, which means, I will not see Alessandro.

Good.

He usually stays in my office, but after what happened yesterday, I told him to stay outside. And I started regretting it because he will be closer to Isabella.

Isabella. I scoff.

A phone ring cuts off my thoughts. I look at the front screen and find Demetrio's number.

"Hello, Demetrio."

"Hello, darling, how are you?"

"I am well, and you?"

"Good. I am calling to tell you that Gino did not say a word at all. I have used everything, he doesn't want to talk."

"That means he's hiding something." I reply and nod to no one in particular.

"Exactly, but I will keep him with me until he says something."

"Okay, thanks a lot Demetrio. I really appreciate it."

"Don't worry about it. Say hi to Annie."

I hang up and place the phone on the table.

It is really weird. Gino came to work for me and didn't tell me who he was at first. He suddenly entered my life and I am sure he didn't do that because he misses me or because he was looking for me and finally found me because if he was looking for me, he would tell me its him immediately.

But what is he hiding?

Why isn't he telling me who killed my parents?

I have to find out.

Grabbing my purse, I open the door and step out. My eyes find Alessandro standing at the corner on my left, scrolling on his phone. Once he sees me, he puts it in his pocket and follows me.

"Where to?"

"Somewhere." I simply say and step into the elevator.

"I saw Isabella crying few minutes ago, did something happen?" He suddenly says.

"And why do you care?" I spat, clearly annoyed from his sudden question.

"I was just asking."

"She deserves it." I say as the elevator pinged, signaling that we arrived at the ground floor.

He doesn't say anything after that, hopefully, he noticed that I am not in the mood to talk neither to him or anyone.

But I still want to ask him about Lily tho.

I make my way towards my car and wait for Alessandro to open the door for me.

When he does, I slid into the back seat with him following me.

"Where to, ma'am?"

"Cemetery." I simply reply, earning a confused look from Alessandro.

Of course, he doesn't know anything about me or my past, he wouldn't know why I am going there.

"Don't worry, I am not going there to kill you." I try to joke, but he didn't laugh.

He was just looking at me weirdly.

"What?" I ask.

"You are different today, what's wrong?"

"Nothing is wrong." I say, a hint of annoyance laced my voice.

Out of nowhere, I was turned around, facing him, with his hands on each side of my waist.

"What are you doing?"

"You have been avoiding me ever since we kissed. We cleared that up, so why are you still ignoring me?" He says with his jaw clenched.

"I am not avoiding you, Alessandro, I am just busy with work." I reply, looking anywhere but not at him.

His hands leaves my body as I adjusted the way I am sitting.

What does he wants me to tell him? That I feel an undeniable attraction towards him? That I want him right here right now? That I hate the way he is making me feel? That I get so mad and jealous when I see him talking to Isabella? That I wish Lily was our daughter?

Wait, I kind of went off. Umm.

The car stops just outside the cemetery, and I prepare myself to step out. Taking my purse, I pull the door open and stepping outside.

I slowly walk to my parent's graves with Alessandro behind me.

"May I ask who are we visiting?" Alessandro's hesitant voice says.

"My parents."

Once I reached their graves, I kneel to their level and place my right hand on each, praying for them.

"I will get you justice, I promise." I mutter, as a tear rolls down my cheek.

I stand back up, whip the fallen tear, and turn around to leave. I glance up and I see Rebecca coming my way.

"Amalia?" Her cracked voice says. She increases her speed until she stood before me.

"Amalia, please, I beg you, listen to me." She desperately says, as tears roll down onto her cheeks.

Looking at her pathetic figure, a smirk make its way on my lips.

You can call me heartless, but I don't care. This person will never ever gain neither my trust nor my sympathy.

"Get out of my way, Rebecca."

"PLEASE, JUST LISTEN FOR GOD'S SAKE!" She yells, making me halt my steps.

How dare she.

"Choose your next words wisely, sister." I threateningly say.

"I am sorry for what happened. I am sorry, Amalia. If I could go back and change everything, I would. I didn't mean to betray you, please forgive me." She sobs.

"Are you saying those words because you need money?" I casually say.

"When did you become this type of person? So heartless, so inconsiderate, MERCILESS!" She yells.

"You are lucky I am ignoring you. If it was someone else, I would have put a bullet in their head." I smile, as I see her face pale.

"And to answer your question, I have always been like this dear sister—but unlike before, I am showing my true colors this time." With that, I turn around and leave, with Alessandro behind me.

The last thing I heard or I think I heard is, "stay away from her she's a devil."

Probably saying that to Alessandro, who else?

———

"May I ask what did she do to you?" Alessandro breaks the silence in the car.

"No, you may not." I rudely reply.

He chuckles.

"Do you think it's funny?"

"Actually, yes, I do—you know I could see through you? I know that you out this hard exterior to push people away, but just so you know, it will never work on me. Do you know why?—" by now, his face is inches away.

"—because you and I both know that we can't stay away from each other, and I know that you cannot wait for me to kiss you again or touch you—I don't know why you are scared to enter a relationship, but I will make sure to find out, and if I didn't, I will make sure to change you." He softly says, as he strokes my left cheek.

I am speechless.

What do you tell a hot, sexy man, if he tells you something like this?

I just nod. Like an idiot. I just nod!!! God!

"Good." A smirk makes its way onto his delicious lips.

We walk side by side and enter the mansion. Annie is standing right in front to greet us.

"Is there anything new?" I ask Annie, as I give her my jacket.

"No, nothing that concerns you, but there is a woman in the living room, who was looking for Alessandro."

"A woman?!" Alessandro and I say at the same time. Mine was a little bit intense tho.

"Who is she?" I ask more directly to Alessandro.

He shrugs and walks to the living room, with me following him.

Who is she? I couldn't get rid of Isabella, and now this?

"Cassie?" He says once he sees her.

"Finally! I have been looking everywhere for you, you little asshat!" She yells and throws herself at him, giving him an intense hug.

I frown as I look at them.

"How did you find this place?" He asks seriously.

"That's for me to know, and you to find out." She smirks. Her eyes settles on me.

"Oh! Where are my manners, Hi, I am Cassie Esposito, this twat's sister." She introduced herself with a bright smile.

"Language, Cas!" He groans, as a smirk makes its way to my lips.

His sister, good.

Plus, I like her. A lot.

"Hello, I am Amalia Ferrari, nice to meet you." I reply kindly.

Why am I good with everyone of his family?

"You are even more gorgeous than the picture."

"Picture?"

"Lily showed me your picture with Alessandro, it's beautiful." She replies, looking between me and Aless.

"Thank you." I smile back.

"I apologize, Amalia. It won't happen again." Alessandro says with a nod.

"I don't mind it at all. In fact, your sister and I have something in common."

"And what is that?" He confusedly asks.

"We both agree that you are a twat." I smile, walking farther into the living room.

I could hear Annie and Cassie laughing from behind.

——I walk to my room and get changed. I am so sleepy and I cannot open my eyes any longer.

Alessandro had left with his sister to his home. I was left with Annie and Gus.

As if on cue, Gus walks into my room, jumping on the bed beside me.

"Hey, baby, did you miss me?" I say, as I pet him.

I love him so much.

My thoughts drift to Alessandro.

He's right, with everything he said in the car. I want him so bad and I want to be with him. This fear that I have towards men has to end at some point, and I want him to do that. I am willing to do it with him because I know I will never find someone like him. Someone who is so kind, selfless, handsome, and gentleman.

He is just so perfect even if his past is a little messed up, tho I don't know a lot about it.

But my life is also messed up, maybe more than him.

Murdered parents, an abusive, cheater boyfriend, and a stupid, backstabbing sister.

Great.

I close my eyes when suddenly my phone rings.

Gosh!

I look at the screen to find an unknown number. What if its something about Gino or my parents?

I quickly hit the accept button, as a video screen showed up.

"Nanny, Amalia, is it you?" A low, sweet, cute voice says.

"Lily?"

"Yes! It's me." She giggles for some unknown reason. "You remember me!"

"Of course, I do, my sweet Lily."

"You are so nice." Her sad voice says, making me frown.

"Why are you saying that?"

"I wish my mother is more like you."

Fuck. That's-

"I am sure she loves you a lot, baby."

"Yeah..."

"How did you get my number, by the way?" I ask, trying to change the subject.

"I stole it from my father's phone when I came last week." She giggles again.

"Good girl." I laugh for the first time in a while.

"Nanny, Amalia?"

"Yes, princess?"

"Will I see you tomorrow? Please say yes."

My heart...

"Of course, you will."

"Okay, then! See you tomorrow." She gives me a kiss and hangs up.

Oh god, I love her. I wish she's my daughter.

I put the phone back on the nightstand, and turn around, facing Gus.

"Why are you looking at me like that?" I frown, as I take his features in.

"Don't worry, I still love you more."

As soon as I said that, he cuddles with me and closes his eyes.

I close mine, and welcome darkness.

———

I am deeply sorry for taking too long to update. I have so much on my mind, and I have so many exams and papers. I hope you understand!

Anyways, what do you think of this chapter?

I hope you liked it

Anyways, I cannot wait to write the next chapter. I love Amalia's and Lily's relationship a lot.

Don't forget to vote and comment! It really means a lot

Word count: 2092

# 11. "You're a Very Ugly Mother."

ALESSANDRO

Hitting the alarm violently, I remove the duvet and stand up, making my way to the bathroom.

I undress and turn on the shower, and adjust the water to reach my liking.

As the water come down, my thoughts go to Amalia.

When I first saw the ad on the internet, I immediately considered working as a bodyguard. One because I would be in Italy close to my daughter, and second, I would take her custody, so we could live together.

The thing is that Amanda is not a good mother. When I first got married to her, I was so in love that I didn't see her true colors sooner. I was blinded by love, and when we had our daughter, everything changed. She changed. She turned into this person who doesn't care about anyone but herself. When I discovered that Lily got lost, I went mad because it wasn't the first time this happens, but the good thing is that I could use this in court.

So when I came to Amalia's house and saw her, I never thought that she would be this young and beautiful. I thought I was working for an old rich rude woman; not that Amalia is not rude, she is, but she's different.

The first my eyes laid on her, I knew that I am in deep shit, and now I know that I was right. This connection that I feel towards her is beyond me. It is so real that I don't think it could ever disappear.

Add on that Lily's love for Amalia. It is as if the universe is giving me a second chance at love, despite Amalia's rough personality, she's an angel, and I think I am the only one; along with Gus, to see this.

Turning off the water, I wrap a towel around my torso, and make my way out.

As I finished wearing my outfit for the day, I hear the door bell.

I quickly make my way towards the door, and pull it open. There she was standing by my doorstep, with our daughter clutching her hand.

"DADDY!" Lily yells, running to me with a crushing hug.

Amanda is just standing there, with a scowl on her face. I was going to say ugly face, but...never mind.

"How are you, baby?" I ask, as I kneel to her level and hug her back. She is wearing a cute pink dress that I know, she's not comfortable in.

Amanda is truly a terrible mother.

"I am good! where is auntie Cassie?-" She asks first, and then says, "-and nanny Amalia?"

"Your aunt is inside, but Amalia is not here, sweetie. She has work." As son as I said that, her face becomes flat, and a pout appeared on her lips.

"But she told me that she will see me today." She looks at the floor, clearly disappointed.

"She did? how?" I ask confusedly.

When did Lily even talk to her, and how? I am sure that I didn't talk to Lily yesterday when I was working, and I didn't hear Amalia talking in my phone or anything.

"I spoke to her on the phone." She mutters and was about to walk inside, when a voice stops her.

"I am here!" Amalia's cheerfully voice says. She walks, bumping Amanda intentionally; which actually made me smile, and hugs Lily with open arms.

"Watch where you're going!" Amanda yells.

Amalia turns around to look at Amanda from head to toe, and a smirk forms on her lips once she saw Amanda's reaction.

"You!"

"Hello, again, Amanda."

"You are fucking her?" Amanda chuckles, as she points at Amalia.

"Watch what you're saying!" I hiss. The last thing I need is Lily hearing those awful words coming from her mother.

"Lily, go inside, sweetie." Amalia says and Lily nods.

Amanda crosses her arms, glaring at Amalia as if did something so awful.

"You didn't answer my question!" She yells annoyingly.

Amalia walks towards me, putting her palm on my chest, and with a flirtatious smile my way, she says, "and what if he is?"

"Disgusting! you went from ME to her? so pathetic." She taunts, as a smirk appears on his lips.

I am beyond mad. How could she say this?

I was about to open my mouth when out of nowhere, it was collided with another. I look down to find Amalia kissing me. I kiss her back.

"Yes, he went from you to me, now I see why." Amalia replies once she breaks the kiss. "Oh, and by the way, you're a very ugly mother."

With that, Amalia grabs my arm inside, shutting the door behind us.

I am still stunned. She just kissed me. I got to taste her lips again. The lips that I thought I'd never ever feel again.

Her lips are addicting and I cannot get enough. I need more.

I grab her arm, turning her around until her chest collided with mine.

"You made a huge mistake by kissing me."

"And why is that?" She innocently replies.

"because now-" I lean close to her ear, "-I will make you beg to kiss me again."

Her breath hitches as she froze in her place. She tries to regain her posture, and she successfully did by saying, "you mean, you will beg me to kiss you again."

"Oh, baby girl, just wait and see."

With that, I walk to the living room where Cassie and Lily are sitting.

~

We are all sitting in the living room, eating ships, and watching Harry Potter movies. Yes, Movie(s). Lily's favorite.

Don't ask, just read.

Amalia is sitting beside Lily on the other side, while I was sitting beside my annoying sister. And I know for a fact that Amalia is sitting far away from me because she cannot handle me. I can even imagine how her heart is beating so fast right now.

I smirk at the thought.

"So, Amalia, what do you do?" Cassie asks, grabbing Amalia's attention.

"I have a travel company." She simply says as Cassie nods.

"That's cool."

"Thanks."

"Daddy, when do I get to live with you?" Lily then asks, breaking my heart in the process.

"Soon, baby." I reply as I look at Amalia to see her nodding as if she's telling me, "I am working on it."

"Nanny Amalia, when I come and live here, can you live with me?"

"Lily." I say warningly.

"I cannot sweetie, but I do live so close from here, you can visit me every single day." Amalia replies sweetly, as she kisses Lily's cheek.

"Really?! did you hear that, daddy?" She says excitedly, earning a nod from me.

"I LOVE YOU!" Lily yells, hugging Amalia.

"Love you too, baby."

I glance at Amalia to see her looking at me. I don't look away, and we just kept looking at each other. Neither of us looking away.

I imagine what could have happened if I married Amalia instead of Amanda. I mean...I am still grateful that I have my Lily, and I wouldn't trade her for the world, but I just wish Amalia is Lily's daughter and not Amanda. Lily already kind of hates her mother, and I don't want that. The problem is that no matter what I say to Lily to change her mind, she is the one whose living with her mother, and she is the one who is taking shit from her everyday.

"As much as I would like to stay with you guys, but I cannot open my eyes any longer, so good night!" Cassie stands up to leave to her room.

"Good night." Amalia and I say in unison.

"I want to sleep too!" Lily announces, standing up to her feet, and following her aunt, but not before kissing Amalia and I.

I was left with Amalia alone.

"Such a sweet girl..." She says with a smile.

"I have never seen her this happy until she met you." I reply, looking at her beautiful eyes. A blush creeped on her face as she looks down.

"I better go."

"Let me take you home."

"You don't have too."

"Actually, I do. I will not let you walk alone at night. I am your bodyguard, remember?" I say earning a chuckle.

We walk side by side, no one is talking as if it is the first time we meet.

When we reach her front door, she turns my way and smiles. "I had fun today. Thanks for having me."

"You're welcome anytime."

"And...I am sorry about the kiss. I did that to anger Amanda." She says.

Disappointment covered my face but soon gone when she says her next words, "But I cannot deny I liked it."

"I'll do it again, if you want." I flirt, leaning in. She doesn't stop me. I stop midway to see if she wants to object or not.

"Alessandro-"

"Mhmm?"

"Can you go any slower?" She groans, slamming her lips onto mine.

This kiss is different than the others. It was demanding and more passionate. Our lips worked so well together as if they finally met after a long time. As if they were waiting each other, even though, not long ago we kissed.

We break the kiss to breathe, and look into each other's eyes.

"Are you okay?" I ask hesitantly, earning a quick nod.

"I am, with you, I am." She smiles.

Thank god!

"As much as I would like to have you in my bed right now, you have to go back to your daughter and sister." She shocks me with her confession.

"I never thought you'd beg me this soon." I tease, as she hits my arm. "Asshole."

"But don't worry, we have so many days to come." I say as I lean in giving her one last gentle kiss.

I turn around to leave, but she stops me.

"Alessandro."

"Yes?"

"Thank you."

"For what?"

"For not giving up on me."

~

Hey guys!

WHAT DO YOU THINK OF ALESSANDRO'S POV? FINALLY!

I hope you liked this chapter, and I am so sorry that it is shorter than the other one, but I just wanted to focus on these things in this chapter.

Also, don't forget to vote, comment, and share! I really appreciate it a lot!

Stay tuned for the next chapter because hell is about to break loose!

Word count: 1734

# 12. "You Look Sexy"

Hey guys! Just wanted to say that this and the next few chapters might be in third person!

Happy reading!

~

Later that night, Amalia couldn't sleep. She was extremely satisfied and happy because she finally let her guard down and trusted someone other than Annie. She had never thought that one day she'd fall in love again, especially after what happened with her ex. She closed the love book a long time ago and didn't think she'd ever open it again.

Tossing right and left, Amalia sat right up, as she glanced at a sleepy Gus. She had been trying to sleep for hours, and no sleep came. She suddenly wished Alessandro would come and sleep beside her.

But how would Gus react? She thought.

She tried to sleep again and this time, she successfully drifted into darkness to dream about Alessandro.

A very hot dream that she wouldn't dare tell anyone about.

~

Walking down the spiral staircase, she received her tea like usual, and made her way to the living room. This time she didn't hear any laugh coming from there like always, and she felt relived.

She then remembered that it's the weekend, and her mind immediately went back to yesterday night. The passionate, demanding kiss. Her heart started beating fast as she remembered how he made her feel just with a kiss.

"How are you, darling?" Annie asked, as she glided her hand along Amalia's back.

"I am good, and you?" Amalia replied, sitting down on one of the couches, and placing her tea on the near table.

"I am well. I want to tell you that I am going out for a little bit."

"Where to?" Amalia asked, clearly shocked that Annie for the first in a long time, wanted to leave the house. She always leaves the house with Amalia, and not alone.

"Somewhere. It's getting really boring staying in the house." Annie explained hesitantly, but tried her best not to show Amalia.

But Amalia knew that Annie was lying, but did not pressure her into telling the truth.

"Fine, but take few guards with you." Amalia gave in, picking up her tea, and taking a small sip.

"Of course."

Suddenly, Amalia's phone pinged signaling that she received a message. She placed her tea carefully on the table, and picked her phone up to see who is it from.

Alessandro: hey, Lia, are you awake?

Lia? Amalia thought. She liked the name, and Alessandro was the first to call her that.

Amalia: hey, Aless, yes, I am, miss me already?

Amalia liked to flirt a lot. She's a master in flirting.

Alessandro: if only you knew what I dreamt last time, you'd certainly know that I don't just miss you.

Amalia couldn't believe what she just read, and blushed from embarrassment. She never knew that such words could make her feel things she hasn't felt in a long time. Not only that, but she also dreamt of Alessandro last night, and she's too shy to say what she dreamt of.

Amalia: would you like to meet to tell me what you dreamt?

After a minute or so, he replied.

Alessandro: yes, but I warn you, I might not keep my hands to myself.

Amalia: I can't say that I might.

With that, Amalia stood up to her feet, and made her way to her bedroom. She was so nervous and wanted to look extremely elegant once she meets with Alessandro.

She has never been this nervous before, and just when she thought she's never return to her old self, she met with Alessandro. The man of her dreams.

As she reached her bedroom, she entered her walk-in closet, and picked up some dresses to pick out from.

A pink or a blue or a red dress? She thought.

She settled with the red one because she wanted to attract Alessandro. She's the devil herself when it comes to seducing men and she loves it. She used to do it when she wanted information from certain people.

She looked at herself in the mirror, and was satisfied. As she left her bedroom, she received another text from Alessandro.

Alessandro: Lily and I are waiting for you in the living room.

With that, Amalia ran down stairs, so eager to see Alessandro and Lily.

As she walked into the living room, Lily ran up to her , hugging her legs. Amalia kneeled to her level and gave her a sweet kiss on the cheeks.

"Hello, princess." Amalia smiled warmly.

"I missed you so much!" Lily yelled happily, hugging her again.

"But we just saw each other yesterday!" Amalia chuckled as she played with Lily's hair.

"I still miss you, don't you want me to miss you? Or you just missed my father?" She pouted, shocking me by her smartness.

"Of course, not! I have missed you more than your father." Amalia shrieked, earning a disapproved look from Alessandro.

His frown says everything.

"How about you go play with Annie and Gus in the backyard, and your father and I will join you after?" Amalia suggested, noticing the corner of Alessandro's mouth curl up, forming a smirk.

Lily nodded happily and turned around and left, following Annie.

After she made sure they were far from her sight, she made her way to Alessandro, who was waiting impatiently on the couch.

Amalia sat down beside Alessandro, closer than she would have before.

"So, are you going to tell me what you dreamt last night?" She seductively said.

"How about you tell me what you dreamt last night." He said, a smirk was visible one his lips, which only made me frown.

"How did-"

"How did I know? Your face says it all, baby girl." He cut me off.

Fuck. She thought. How could he tell I dreamt of him from my face?

"I didn't dream of you last night." She snapped, swallowing hard. Never in her lifetime had she ever felt like this. She always knew how to control herself, yet she cannot do that with him.

She's vulnerable with him.

"Really?" He said, as his hand reached her thigh, drawing circles dangerously close to that area that She wanted to be touched in so badly.

"Uha.."

"Let me tell you about my dream then. Maybe it'll refresh your memory about yours." His smirk grew wider. "Oh, and by the way, you look sexy." He murmurs, making her blush.

Alessandro went on telling her about his dream, and how she was enjoying it as her moans and screams were everywhere.

The deeper he goes, the deeper her blush becomes, and he was enjoying that, a lot.

She couldn't look him in the eyes when he finished telling her about his crazy dream. Her breathing got harder and her body felt like it's on fire.

He took her by the waist, placing her on his lap, straddling him. He rounded his arms around her waist, pushing her closer as their chests touched.

"Now, do you remember what you dreamt of me?" He teased, making her blush more if that's even possible.

She couldn't believe that the once evil Amalia is sitting here on a man's lap, and blushing hard.

"I dreamt...that you and I... were having sex." She finally said, keeping away the part where she later found that she's pregnant.

She didn't want to say that not because she didn't want it to happen, but because she doesn't want to embarrass herself. What if he doesn't want babies with me? She thought. What if he leaves me?

She knew that it was just a dream, but a part of her wished it was real.

"You know..." he started, his hands caressing her back gently. "I would like to know the details, but I'll let it go as you cannot breathe. Are you hot?" He teased her even more. He knew that she's very unstable right now, and only with one touch she'd melt away.

He knew the affect he had on her, and he wanted to let her know that.

She was about to say something when his lips smashed onto hers, pushing her even closer to his chest. His hands went to her ass cheeks, cupping them gently, while she moaned into the kiss. To her, every kiss is different. She enjoyed it a lot. She wanted more.

She couldn't get enough.

~The next day

"Ezekiel, what's for lunch?" Amalia asked her chef with a smile on her face that confused Ezekiel. He sees her smile for the first time, and he couldn't believe his eyes.

"Chicken Alfredo, Ms. Ferrari." He said, with a bright smile.

"Perfect." She replied and left to the living room to drink her tea.

As she walked into the living room, she spotted Isabella. Alessandro was nowhere to be seen.

"Good morning, Ms. Ferrari!"

"Hello, Isabella. How's everything going at the company?" Amalia asked, sitting on the couch, and grabbing the newspaper.

"Everything is good. I finished everything you told me to do." She replied hesitantly.

"Tell me."

"Tell you what?"

"What do you want."

"I-I don't want anything." Isabella replied as she swallowed hard.

"Tell me." Amalia asked again, impatiently this time.

"Could I have few days off? Please."

"You're lucky I am in a good mood. You can take 5."

"5?! Thank you so much." She said gratefully with a bright smile on her smile.

Amalia just nodded and focused her attention to the newspaper at hand.

Today's news

A body was found dead at Lago di Balancino in the afternoon. Authorities believe that the man is to be Gino Garcia, and has been dead since yesterday night with three bullets in the head. The police believe that the deceased had killed himself in an attempt of suicide.

Fuck! Amalia thought.

She quickly snatched her phone from the near table, and looked for Demetrio's number.

"Hello?"

"What the hell happened? Why is Gino dead?" She quickly asked, annoyance laced her voice.

"It's a long story, but he killed himself." Demetrio replied lazily.

"Wasn't he locked up? How did he run away?"

"He didn't. He killed himself while he was locked up. When one of my men was delivering a tray of food, he attacked him and took his gun. He somehow managed to get free from the chains." Demetrio explained.

"I cannot believe this...what are we going to do? I am back to square one." She replied.

"Don't worry, we'll figure it out." He assured her.

With that, she hung up.

~

Hey guys!!!! I hope you liked this chapter! I am so excited for the next chapters as some action will finally happen!

How do you like Amalia's and Alessandro's relationship? I know it escalated quickly, but I didn't want to postpone it any longer.

Also, do you think Annie is hiding something or no? If yes, what?

Don't forget to vote, comment, and share  it really means a lot

Word count: 1825

# 13. "I Don't Trust Him"

Monday.

Removing the duvet that covered her creamy skin, Amalia walks to the bathroom to start the day. Ever since she spoke with Demetrio two days ago about Gino, she has made plans to visit Florence to talk with Demetrio, and that's going to be tomorrow.

Today is the circle day. A new member has joined, and it is mandatory for every member to attend to meet with this new member. It is rarely for any new members to join, and that's what concerned Amalia. Where did this new elite come from? She thought.

She has never heard of his name before in the marketplace, and that raised suspicions in her.

Circling her thumb and pointy around the shower head, she takes it off the hanger and cleans off the soap that covered her body.

After she finished, she walked outside, wrapping a towel around her body.

For first impressions, she loved making a statement, and she did that with her outfit. She always chooses something that would intimidate others, just like she did when she met Isabella and Alessandro. To her, perfect clothing is power.

Settling upon the dark maroon blazer set, she out it on. A simple, yet sultry makeup look covered her face.

Walking downstairs, she was met with Annie and her tea.

"Buongiorno, il mio amore." Annie greets, her voice filled with warmth.

"Buongiorno, mamma." Amalia replies back, as she took the cup of tea from her mother, and walking into the living room to greet the rest.

"Good morning, Alessandro." Amalia smiles, as she reaches for a kiss, and being granted one.

"Morning, my love." He smirks, giving in to the kiss.

"Sorry to interrupt your little moment, but where is Isabella?" Annie says.

"She's kn a break." Amalia replies, sitting on the couch, and motioning for Alessandro to do the same.

"We have to leave to Florence tomorrow. I have to meet with Demetrio and discuss Gino. I still cannot believe he died without giving useful information." Amalia explains, huffing in the process.

"When are we leaving?" Alessandro asks.

"Tomorrow morning."

Amalia picks up her cup of tea, taking a lingering sip before putting it back down. She had always loved tea. It is one of her favorite hot drinks on Earth.

Looking between Annie and Alessandro, she farrows her eyebrows, as she saw something weird between them.

"What is it?"

"What is what?" Alessandro asks, confusedly.

"There is something between the two of you that you are hiding. What is it?" She presses.

"There's nothing, sweetie." Annie replies this time. Amalia was not convinced, but she let it slip this time.

"Anyways, we have to leave. I have a meeting with the circle." Amalia announces, glancing at Alessandro, who nodded in approval.

After kissing Annie goodbye, Amalia and Alessandro stroll out the front door. The fresh breeze touched Amalia's skin as she walked to the car.

"By the way, Lily says hi and told me to give you a kiss." Alessandro suddenly says once they got seated.

She gave him a side glance and the corners of her lips lifted into a smirk.

"Where do you want to give the kiss this time?" He says, making her blush like a Rose.

"Just the cheek." She replies, knowing that he's going to be disappointed, and surely, the look on his face proved her point.

"Fine, fine. Just kiss me anywhere you want." She bites her bottom lip, averting her eyes so she doesn't look at him.

"Anywhere?" He smirks, as he got closer.

"Slow down, pretty boy. You got it all wrong." He chuckles once she says that.

"Ugh, fine." He rolls his eyes, as he pressed his lips on her cheek, causing her to get disappointed this time.

The driver arrived at the building where the circle is held in. Amalia was not looking forward to the meeting at all. Not only does she has tolerate her members, but she has to greet and tolerate the new one.

Stepping out of the car, Alessandro and Amalia walk side by side to the building. Alessandro's hand was pressed firmly on his holster incase an attack happens. He didn't trust the circle, just like Amalia.

As they reached the top floor, the secretary opens the meeting room for them, as it can only be opened by few people with a hand print. Amalia could have dine that, but the secretary did it instead out of respect.

Even though Amalia didn't like it. She knew she could do things on her own, and yet, this girl still does it. Amalia doesn't understand why, but she thought maybe it's out of respect.

"Greetings." Amalia greets everyone, as she makes her way towards her seat. Her eyes wandered around the seaters, hoping to find this 'new' member. Once her eyes settled on him, she smiles.

"Welcome to the circle, Mr.?—"

"Alba. Cintinio Alba." He replies with a smile.

"Nice to meet you. I am Amalia Ferrari."

"It's a pleasure." He nods.

Alessandro didn't like this man, not in one bit. It wasn't that he was jealous ir anything, but he didn't trust him. He felt that this man is trouble, and was determined to prove that.

Amalia could sense Alessandro's narrowed eyes that sent daggers to the new man. She didn't know if it was jealousy or not, but she too was determined to know why is he acting weird.

"So, what do you do?" One of my colleagues asks, aiming the question at Mr. Alba.

"I am a businessman. I have a chain of hotels and clubs all over the world." He replies proudly.

"That's impressive." Amalia comments, nodding in the process.

"Thank you." He nods back.

For the next two hours, they kept knowing each other. Alba discovered that Amalia has a travel company, and promised to use her company when he travels again. Amalia didn't see anything wrong with the man, or any red flags. She, however, did know that he was lying when he told her that he'd never been to Italy before today, and that's a lie because Amalia swore that she saw him somewhere here in Italy before.

And Amalia never forgets a face when she sees it, but why did he lie? She thought.

Shaking hands with Cintinio, Amalia leaves the meeting with Alessandro trailing behind her. Once they got into the car, Alessandro did not waste a moment to talk about Alba.

"I don't like him. He's fishy."

"Why? I thought he was good." Amalia bites back her laugh. She wanted to see what Alessandro is trying to imply.

"I don't trust him. What if he's here to target you?" He suggests.

"Not everyone is after me. Besides, there hasn't been any attack on me, so I feel they forgot about it."

"Don't let your guard down. They will hunt you down when you are vulnerable. Do not trust anyone." He warns, earning a nod from his girlfriend.

Amalia will forever be grateful for Alessandro. She knew she got lucky this time and she's happy that she had met him.

"By the way, I have to tell you something." She starts nervously.

"What is it?" Alessandro replies. He was a bit nervous from what she was about to say. What if she wanted to break-up with me? He thought.

"Remember our first meeting?—" She starts, earning a nod, "—it wasn't our first."

"What do you mean? Have we met before?" Surprise covered Alessandro's features. He did not expect that at all.

"We met 6 years ago when I was living for a while in England—you were actually my neighbor." Amalia chuckles, as she remembers her tiny crush on Alessandro.

"I was still married at that time." He replies, thinking in the process.

"Yeah, I remember. I kind of had a crush on you." She says shyly.

"How come I never saw you?" He farrows his eyes-brows.

"You were too blinded by miss perfect." Amalia rolls her eyes, jealous that he was married to that woman and not her.

A smirk appeared on his face, as he got closer to her, wrapping his arms around her waist, lifting her up, and placing her on his lap. This move made her cheeks burn in embarrassment.

"Are you jealous?" He murmured, as he breathed her scent. He couldn't get enough of her.

"Yes." She breathed out, not noticing the breath she was holding. She had no problem in admitting she was jealous because she was, and she wanted him to know.

Alessandro was amused by her honesty and that made him love her even more.

"Good." He kisses her shoulder. "How about we go on vacation after meeting with Demetrio? Just the two of us." He whispers the last part.

She turns to face him, and a grin covered her lips. "I don't mind."

——

This is chapter eleven you guys! I hope you like it. I know, I know, it is a very short chapter and I am so sorry for that, but believe me when I say that I had so much trouble in writing this chapter. The reason I didn't update any sooner wasn't only because I was busy with school work, but also, because I didn't know what to write. I tried so hard to write this chapter sooner, but I couldn't. Sorry for that.

Anyways, what do you think of the chapter? 1- what do you think of Cintinio Alba?2- why do you think Amalia told Alessandro that they met before?

Follow me on Instagram AND please don't forget to vote, comment, and share. It really means a lot

# 14. "We Need to Hide"

The sun was shinning as the plane was flying to its destination, Florence. Amalia and Alessandro were going to Florence to visit Demetrio and discuss the Gino incident. It was a confusing case to Amalia, as she couldn't wrap her head around what had happened to Gino. She truly believed that Demetrio had nothing to do with it because she trusted him, but she didn't believe that Gino would kill himself. Maybe it's what Demetrio thinks? She thought. Amalia refused to be the reason Gino is dead, even though she could careless.

The flight-attendant brought the duo drinks and snacks to enjoy till they arrive to Florence. As the drinks were being placed on the table, they hit the floor with a loud smash. It wasn't that the flight-attendant intentionally or non-intentionally dropped them, but it was the plane that suddenly swayed right and left.

"What's happening?" Amalia asks, her heart dropped along with the plane.

Alessandro held onto his boss tightly, making sure she doesn't get hurt. The plane was landing for some unknown reason and he knew the feeling too well, as he had experienced it before when he was at war.

"Don't worry, we'll be fine." He says, trying to soothe her.

"Attention everyone, due to technical issues, we have to land at the nearest island, which is Capri." The pilot announced.

"There's something wrong." Amalia mumbles, as she looked around. "I think someone is trying to kill us." She adds.

"Are you sure?" Alessandro asks.

"Before we left Sicily, I saw a car following us, but I thought it was just a coincidence. I didn't think that it might be an attacker."

"Why didn't you tell me?" He groans.

"I didn't think it was something." She rolls her eyes.

"But what does that have to do with the plane?" The flight-attendant asks. Amalia and Alessandro glare at him, not liking that he was listening to their conversation.

The plane suddenly landed with a thud. As soon as the plane had stopped, the door was opened, and everyone made their way out. The plane had landed somewhere along the beach.

It was a miracle they survived.

As they made their way out, gunshots were fired startling everyone.

"We need to hide!" Alessandro announces, taking Amalia's hand and running for their lives. They ran into the forest, as trees passed around them. They could hear people following them, but thankfully, they weren't gaining on them. Luckily for Amalia, she wasn't wearing heels, and that's the first time it happened because Alessandro insisted she wore something casual this time. He loved her glam self, but he wanted to see her casual side too.

They took a turn, arriving at a huge waterfall. There was nowhere else they could go, as they reached the end of the way. They looked behind and found the men approaching with guns in their hands. There was nothing in Alessandro's head other than to take Amalia's hand and jump down. He knew that the men wouldn't jump because in reality, no one would.

"Do you trust me?" He asks, holding her hand.

"Yes, why?"

He didn't reply and just tightened his grip, and jumped down. Amalia's screams filled the area, as she didn't think Alessandro would jump off a waterfall, taking her with him. As soon as they hit the water, Amalia was long out of it, but Alessandro's hand was still attached with her as he could not let it go. He swam to the surface, with her beside him. He held onto her lifeless body as they reached to the land. He took an immediate action, trying to give her oxygen. Once he did that, she opened her eyes coughing the water out of her lungs.

"You okay?" Alessandro's worried voice asks.

"Yes." She breathlessly replies.

He lifted her up in a bridal style and walked farther into the forest. She clung onto him tightly, as if her life depended on him. After five minutes, Alessandro saw a small, wooden, round house. He glanced around their surroundings, making sure there wasn't anyone. Once he was sure, he made his way inside. The small, tiny house was basic.

There was a small bed on the corner, a door that probably connected to the bathroom, and a small chair. He figured this was a place where someone was prisoned in. He knew there were a lot of mafias in Italy, and this seemed like the perfect, remote place to guard someone in.

"Fuck, I didn't know you'd jump down, let along with me." Amalia mutters, putting her hair out if the way.

"I had too, or else, we would be dead." He replies, sitting beside her on the bed.

"We are alone, we need to somehow call Demetrio." Amalia suggests.

"We can't. We don't have a phone. Plus, they might be tracking our phones." He replies, shaking his head.

"Then, what are we going to do?"

"We have to stay here for few hours, and then, we can leave. I just hope they won't find us."

"Me too."

Amalia snuggled onto Alessandro, seeking warmness. Just like she had never thought she will ever find love again, she had never thought she'd find safety and comfort in someone too. It was something new to her, but it wasn't scary like she thought. Before Alessandro, all she could ever think about is power and money. She loved control and loved to manipulate those around her, even Annie. After what happened with her ex and with her sister, Amalia changed for the worst. Being betrayed by your loved ones is not easy, especially when your sister is amongst them.

The night came and Amalia slept her worries away. Alessandro busied himself to stay awake, playing with Amalia's hair. He had to stay awake to make sure no one comes in. He knew that from this moment, everything is going to change. Amalia is even more in dangerous than he could ever thought. She needs protection 24/7, and might always be on the run. Those people who are after her were willing to take the plan down; something that will grab the authorities' attention, even though they failed as the pilot took control of the plane and landed it safely. That's how much they wanted Amalia dead.

The next day, Amalia woke up with a headache. She looked around her surroundings and didn't find Alessandro. Her heart clenched as she thought of many scenarios, one him being killed, or the other, he left her. But she knew too well that he wouldn't do that. She immediately stood up, carefully walking outside the tiny house. She glanced around the trees, hoping to find Alessandro. She suddenly heard a noise coming from behind the house. She slowly walked towards the sound, and found Alessandro talking with a chained man.

"What's happening here?" Amalia asks.

"Found him roaming this morning. He is one of the men who followed us." He replies.

As soon as Amalia heard that, she strolled towards the man, and threw a punch on his face. She was so pissed that she had to go through all of this because of these men. The man groaned in pain, as he tried to hold his nose, but failed miserably.

"Who sent you?" Amalia asks, holding his neck tightly.

The man didn't utter a word and that angered Amalia. She walked towards Alessandro, took his gun from his holster, and walked back aiming the gun at the man. She was so fed up to an extent that she would pull the trigger and kill the man because she had enough.

"Tell. Me." She says rather dangerously.

A look of fear and surprise covered the man's features. It would seem that he was told Amalia wouldn't hurt a fly, yet here she is, aiming the gun at him without blinking.

She took the safety off, ready to shoot when the man uttered the words she had been waiting. "Please, don't shoot! I will tell you." The man says.

"Who?"

"Look, I do not know who exactly is behind all of this, but a man found me and told me to kill you for 1 million dollars, and I agreed. I didn't even know you before today."

Amalia didn't like his response and thought of shooting him, but she knew she'd regret that later, even if he was going to kill her. She gave the gun back to its owner, and walked back to the house. Alessandro followed her shortly after making sure the ropes were intact.

"Are you okay?" Alessandro asks, as soon as he entered the house.

"I am not. We have to leave to Florence and meet with Demetrio. We are not safe anymore." She replies, huffing in this process.

"Come on, let's go."

"What about the man at the back?"

"He'll stay...until someone finds him." Alessandro smirks, taking her hand, and walking out.

-------

So guys! here is chapter fourteen! I hope you liked this chapter. Things in the next chapter are going to be fireeee, are you ready?

So, who do you think is behind the attack?

Do you think Amalia and Alessandro will make it to Florence?

Tell me your thoughts!

Also, I am sorry for the short chapters these days, but I feel I cannot write a long one anymore, I don't know why.

Another thing, do you miss their POVs? or you like the third person?

Word count: 1568

# 15. Florence

AMALIA

"Are you sure it's the right way?" I ask, as I walk carefully over the rocks. Alessandro and I have been walking for hours in this forest, and haven't been lucky to finding the main town. The sun is almost setting down.

"Not sure, but I feel we are close to the main street." He replies hesitantly, as I groan in pain and sadness. I just want to get to Florence.

As we walk, we heard few growls here and there, and that made me stick close to Alessandro, holding his arm for safety. I am just glad that I am not alone here and I have Alessandro because if he wasn't here, I am sure I would be dead a long time ago. We passed the beautiful dark green tress as we walked, and saw a bunch of different kinds of birds resting on the branches. They looked beautiful.

After few more hours of walking, we finally reached the main road. It was dark now, but thankfully, someone agreed to take us to Capri's train station. We didn't want to go to the airport because we didn't want to draw attention. It is clear now that I am not safe and I am on the run. I am concerned with Annie and if she's safe. That's why I need to reach Florence to ask Demetrio for his help and know more about Gino.

We booked a train ticket and the train will leave in two hours. Luckily, it is only four and half hours to reach Florence by train. I just hope we don't encounter any more men.

As we wait, Alessandro bought some bagels for us to eat. I love bagels, a lot. It reminds me of old time with my parents when we used to go to the park and play there. I miss those old gold days.

"Are you okay?" Alessandro asks, sitting beside me on the bench, and handing me the bagel.

"I am. I am just concerned with Annie. What if they did something to her?" I ask nervously.

"Don't worry. I am sure she's okay. Besides, there are a lot of body-guards guarding the house." He assures me. I feel better when he said that. I am sure she's okay.

"I hope so." I sighed.

In two hours, the train arrived and they started calling for everyone to go on board. We made our way to our flat number that was written on our ticket, and hopped into the train. We took our seats; which were beside each other, and made sure to not look suspicious. We glanced around a bit, making sure no ones was watching or spying on us.

I took Alessandro's hand in mine, and never felt more safe. He is my safe place. I closed my eyes, knowing that I am safe with Alessandro, as darkness engulfed me.

————————————

We gave the taxi driver Demetrio's address and sped off. We arrived to Florence few minutes ago safely. Thank god. We didn't see anyone else trying to kill us, yet. Alessandro stayed beside me the whole time and never once left me alone. Even when he went to buy something to eat, he took me with him. He couldn't leave me alone, and honestly, I would not leave him too.

After half an hour, we have arrived to Demetrio's house. I remember the last time I came here, and that was when I dumped Gino. I can't help but feel a little bit if guilt that I was the reason my cousin is dead, but then again, he wasn't the Gino I knew. He hid a lot of secrets that I have yet to discover.

"Thank you." I thank the taxi driver, as Alessandro hand him some money. I didn't have anything with me. No cell phone or money. I thank god Alessandro had some in his pockets.

I knock on the door, waiting impatiently for someone to open it. After few seconds, the door opened.

"Fuck! Where have you been?" Demetrio yells, relief covered his face once he saw us.

"We'll explain, but let us come in first." I reply in a hurry. We enter the house and make our way to the familiar living room. As soon as I step my foot into the living room, I hear familiar voices.

Annie?

"Annie?" I voice my thoughts, gaining her attention.

"Oh my god! Thank god you are okay!" She replies, hugging my tightly. "Have you got any idea how much worried I was?"

"What happened? Why ate you here?"

"They attacked the house, I had to leave." She replies sadly.

"Oh god, are you okay?" I ask, grabbing both of her shoulders.

"I am now that you are. What happened?"

Alessandro and I sat down and explained everything that had happened. From the departure till now. They were shocked to hear what happened, but thankful that nothing happened to us.

"I can't believe that happened." Demetrio grunts. "You are in danger, now."

"I know..." I sigh. I glance at Demetrio, signaling that we should talk alone. He nods and motions for me to follow him. I left Alessandro with Leila and Annie, and followed Demetrio to his office. Once we reached, he opens the door and lets me in.

"We have to talk about Gino. What happened?" I asks, in a demanding voice.

He sighs and replies, "if only I knew. I was i interrogating him and when I left, he was still chained to the table. I am not sure, but I guess he wanted to go to the bathroom because after few minutes, I heard a gun shot in the basement. When I went back there, I saw the bodyguard's body on the floor. Gino was nowhere to be seen. I later concluded that there was a spy between us who helped him out. However, just an hour later, we heard the new of his death.

The police claimed that it was a suicide, but I do not think so." He explains.

"Do you think the people he worked for killed him? Maybe they were afraid he would say something." I ask.

"There's a 90% chance of that." He nods, approvingly.

I was about to say something else, but Leila's screams were heard, making us jolt up and run towards the living room. When we arrived, the scene I saw before me broke my heart.

There was Annie on the floor unconscious. Her mouth was covered with white foam.

"What happened?" I ask, running towards my mother.

"She just collapsed." Leila replies.

"Call the doctor!" I yell.

——

# 16. Annie

AMALIA

Heartbreak.

That's what I am feeling currently. Seeing your loved ones on a hospital bed unconscious is not easy. I have tried to never ever think of this moment. I never thought about Annie getting ill because if I did, I would be 24/7 worried and scared. Here she was, lying on the soft white sheets, as the nurse checked up on her. Yesterday, she fell unconscious all of a sudden, without a warning. We didn't know what happened, but now we do.

Annie is ill. She's sick. The doctor said she has some type of cancer that I can't really pronounce. It appeared that when she used to go out of the house, it was only to check up on her illness. I didn't know anything of that because she didn't tell me, and it hurts to think that she might have died without saying goodbye. The cancer is in stage three and the doctor believes that she won't live long. The amount of emotions I am feeing is beyond words. After my parent's death,

I never cared about anyone else. The only person I cared about was Annie. She is my life and just the thought of losing her right now, hurts a lot.

"She needs to rest." The doctor said. Alessandro and I were in her room, hoping for her to just open her eyes. We left her room and went to where Demetrio and Leila were staying.

"Thank you for everything." I say, as soon as I saw them. Without Demetrio, I couldn't have lived this long. He is like a father figure to me and I will forever be grateful for him.

"Don't thank me. You are family." He replies, giving me a side hug.

"You better go rest. I prepared an extra room for you two." Leila says.

We thanked her and walked to the room she told us about. As much as this is the last thing I want to do, I can't help but feel tired and drained. Staying a full night in the woods didn't help either. That stiff bed almost broke my back.

"Are you okay, baby?" Alessandro softly asks, stroking my cheek. I leaned in at his touch. It was addicting.

"I am not, but I will." I nod, kissing him on the cheek. He was the only person that's keeping me from losing my mind. At this point, I cannot imagine life without him. He is the only one left.

All of a sudden, the bed dipped. I looked to my left to find Gus. Oh, I forgot to mention that Annie managed to take him with her. I don't want to even think of what could have happened if he didn't make it out.

"Hey, baby." I coed, giving him a kiss on the head.

"I get jealous, by the way." Alessandro teases. I know he was trying to make me feel better, which it did.

I chuckle.

"Really?" I grin, earning a nod.

I smirk and lean in to give him a kiss on the lips. As soon as my lips touched his, butterflies flew in my stomach, giving me a wonderful feelings. I can't describe it, but the love I have for him is beyond words.

"Mhmm." He moaned into the kiss. At this point, we forgot that Gus was with us. We kept kissing like there was no tomorrow. We couldn't get away from each other as if, if we did, we could die.

We broke the kiss, taking deep breaths, and just looking into each other's eyes. The way he makes me feel is beyond description. I cannot even think of what he makes me feel. The way he hold me...the way he talks to me... the way he kisses me, is really beyond anything I have ever experienced in my whole life. I pray to god that he's mind forever.

"I don't know what would I do without Annie." I comment sadly. As much as I want to cherish this moment, my thoughts are clouded by Annie's, and I cannot get my head to think about anything else. She's my mother after all.

"I will be here, with you. You are not alone—besides, you are going to do just fine, I am sure of that." He says, hugging my tightly.

"Don't leave me, ever." I say, looking into his beautiful blue eyes, as he nods. "Never."

——The next day, we were sitting in the living room when Mia; Demetrio's daughter, came in. She looked quite grown. I haven't seen her in a while.

"Did the doctor say anything?" Demetrio asks his daughter.

"No. Annie is still the same as yesterday." She replies. A look of pity covered her stunning brown eyes.

I didn't want to say anything. Actually...I wanted to scream so loud, but I didn't. I couldn't.

"Thank you, Demetrio. For everything."

"Don't thank me, Amalia. You are family." He gives me a weak smile. I know I said this so many times before, but I will always be grateful for Demetrio, especially now that my home is destroyed and I have to stay here for a while.

"When are you going back to America?" I ask. I remember him telling me that he was going back to Galena with his family last week, but he didn't.

"Not sure, yet. Let's see how we could solve all of this now." He replies, referring to my situation. I suddenly feel bad because I held him here in Florence when he wanted to go back to his home.

"Don't give me that look and don't feel bad" he rolls his eyes.

How the fuck did he knew?

"I can read you like a book." He smiles.

I decided to tease him and make him angry since I know this topic irritate him.

"So, Mia, when is the wedding?—and are you moving out somewhere else?" I ask, as I glance at Demetrio's face, which by the way, turned red.

"Uhh—it should be this year—and yeah, we are thinking of moving out." She hesitantly replies, looking at her father for assurance.

"Mhm, that's wonderful!"

"Enough! About this bullshit, we can talk about it later." Demetrio growls, making Mia and I laugh uncontrollably. He looks so funny when he gets angry.

For those of you who don't know, Demetrio's daughter is engaged to this guy named River. Demetrio loves River a lot, but the fact that his daughter is with someone and is going to marry soon, and move out, irritates him. He wants his daughter to be all for him and his wife. She's his little baby and will always be. So, when anyone talks about Mia's relationship, he gets worked up, and it is so funny.

"Fine." I playfully roll my eyes.

"What about you?—when are you getting married?" Leila asks with a smirk, as she wiggles her eyebrows.

All the oxygen left my body when I heard that because Alessandro was here with us, listening to everything, and I cannot even reply because we never talked about it. What if he doesn't want to marry me? But why wouldn't he want to? I am his girlfriend, right?

I am dying to know.

I was about to respond with a "I am not sure," when Alessandro blessed us all with a, "very soon."

I choked on my saliva once I heard that, earning an amused look from him. He had this smirk that said, "I know you want to marry me."

Of course! I want to marry you, you idiot

Is it normal that I love him so much?

"Y-yeah...very s-soon." I stuttered like a child, not looking into anyone's eyes.

It was nice that we had this conversation. It took my mind off Annie a little bit, but it made me feel terrible. I didn't want to sit here and have fun when she was lying on that death bed, waiting for her moment to go. I didn't want to watch her go, but I knew I have to stay beside her. So, I decided to go to her room and sit beside her. Hopefully, she wakes up and sees me beside her.

I stood up, telling everyone that I an going to Annie's room, and made my way there. I told Alessandro to stay downstairs because he really didn't have to follow me everywhere. As much as I want him to be glued to me 24/7, it is not fair to him.

I opened the door to where Annie is staying, and made my way in. The sound of the monitor was beeping slowly, indicating that she's in good health...I guess.

I grabbed a chair slowly towards her bed, and plopped myself down. She looked angelic while asleep. Suddenly, my mind drifted to my sister. I remember how much Annie wanted me to forgive Rebecca, was it because she knew that she was going to die, and wanted to see us back together before she leaves this cruel world? I am not so sure anymore...

But she has to know that it is not easy for me to forgive someone who had betrayed me. She betrayed me with my ex-boyfriend. The same boyfriend who kept me hospitalized for five months. The same boyfriend my sister stood with when I told her what he did. She didn't believe me. She was too consumed by the love that she thought she had for him. She was too much fooled by him. And again, I don't blame her because I was too. He had this thing where he could make you do, see, and feel things that he wanted.

"Oh, mamma, I wish you told me. I wish I had spent more time with you." A tear escaped my eye, landing my on cheek.

If this has taught me anything, it was to cherish every moment with your loved ones. I cannot believe that I was too consumed by the circle and power, that I forgot to spend time with my mamma. She is my everything. My only family left.

I took her hand in my and squeezed. I wanted her to know that I am here beside her, and that I am not leaving her side. Never!

"I promise you, I will change." Those were my last words to her before the monitor beeped loudly, indicating that something was wrong with her. I yelled for the doctors to come, and the door immediately flew open. A doctor and a nurse entered and asked me to leave. Trust me, I didn't want to leave, but they left me no choice.

I was a crying mess. Alessandro, Demetrio, and Leila ran my way asking questions that I couldn't answer.

I too, didn't know what was happening to Annie.

"She's going to die!" I sob, hugging Alessandro tightly. I didn't want him to leave my side at all. All I wanted was for him to hug me tighter, and tell me that it is going to be okay.

"I am here, baby." He kisses the too of my head.

Few minutes had passed when the door flew open, revealing the doctor.

"I am deeply sorry to say this—but we couldn't do anything else. May she rest in peace."

I fell to the floor upon hearing the news. The news were like a poison to me. I knew that she wasn't going to live longer, but I never expected it to be so soon. I was just with her fee minutes ago, and she was good, as if when she heard me, she couldn't take it and died. Was I the reason?

"You aren't." Demetrio whispers, as he hugged me. He knew me too well.

Annie is dead and now, I am alone.

————————Hey guys! I hope you liked this chapter! To be honest, I dreaded writing it and it is not one of my favorites, but it had to be written! I am extremely sorry for updating super late :(

To be honest, I was heavily thinking of stopping this story. For some reason, I am not motivated to write it, but I know that this thing happens to me with every story when it reaches the end. There are still many chapters left for this story so do not worry. I will continue writing it until I finish it.

Also, for my next story, I don't want to start it and update every once in a while, so I will wait until I fully or semi fully write it and then upload it. I know I always say that, but this time I want to try it. I have to

Thanks for being patient and sorry for updating late again

Word count: 2132

# 17. Lily

AMALIA

A week had passed since Annie death, and since then, we have stayed with the González's. My home was not safe and I couldn't go back there. I received few emails from the circle, but I didn't reply to any. I knew they were in on whatever happened to me. They were after me and I couldn't go back there. Sicily was now a very dangerous place for me.

"Have you talked to Lily?" I ask, sitting beside Alessandro.

"Yes, I just talked to her. She says hi." He replies with a smile.

"Didn't she want a kiss?" I shyly ask. I wanted him to kiss my neck so bad.

"If you want me to kiss you so bad, all you gotta do is ask, baby." He smirks once he saw the blush on my cheeks. He leaned in and kissed my neck, a slow, burning kiss. It felt so good.

"By the way, I have asked Amanda to come to Florence and bring Lily. I want to keep her beside me."

"Yes, of course. No problem." I reply happily. I was so excited to see that cutie again.

Even though, I am not in the nicest mindset right now, but I could get better with Lily around. I just need a fresh air and someone to take my mind off Annie. I still cannot believe that she's gone and worse, that she didn't tell me about her disease. I didn't even get to say goodbye. I am sure she did that for a reason.

And then again, my mind drifts to what she had been telling me for years, to talk to my sister again. She clearly knew that she was dying and wanted to see me with my sister again before she does, and I didn't grant her her wish. I was so selfish, but I didn't even know.

That's not an excuse too...

Suddenly, a phone rings. Alessandro's

"Yes, Amanda, did you arrive?" Alessandro says, waiting for her reply. Suddenly, his face turns hard and his eyes widen.

"WHERE ARE YOU?" He yells through the phone. He nods involuntarily and hangs up.

"What happened?" Demetrio and I ask at the same time. Demetrio had just walked into the room.

"Lily...they took Lily." He says, shocking us.

My heart started beating fast, the oxygen was leaving my body, and I couldn't think straight. Is that what being afraid is? You get frozen in your place and can't move at all? While your heart keep bumping onto your chest rapidly, as if it wants to get out.

Lily...they took her because of me.

Alessandro grabbed his car keys without saying another word and left the house. I ran after him, wanting to go with him, but I couldn't keep up with him. He was too fast.

"Alessandro!" I yell after him.

"Amalia, get in the car!" Demetrio calls, grabbing my attention. I walked to his car and hopped in. He turned the engine on and sped after Alessandro.

Sandro was going to do something reckless and ai couldn't leave him alone, especially when it is not his mess but mine. I got him into this...it is my fault that Lily has been kidnapped.

I hope she's okay...

Alessandro's car stopped and we did too. We hopped out and walked after him. Amanda was standing by the road, crying her eyes out. This is the first time I see her in this position. Even when her daughter was lost few months ago when I found her, she didn't cry like that.

"Who took her!" Alessandro yells.

"Some men! They said that you are going to pay the price because of HER!" She cries and points at me.

"Did they say who they were?" I ask.

"Are you stupid? Of course, they wouldn't tell me! They just took her!" She cries again. I didn't say anything because it is my fault and because she just saw her daughter get kidnapped in front of her and couldn't do anything about it. Otherwise, I would have killed her right here right now.

"Alessandro! Please get her back!" She cries more, hugging him in the process. I didn't like it one bit, but I couldn't do anything about it.

"We will find her." He replies, hugging her back lightly.

All of a sudden, I get a phone call, grabbing everyone's attention. It was an unknown number and I knew they were the kidnappers.

I quickly answered it.

"Who are you?" I demand.

"Well, well, hello, "queen Amalia."" The voice mocks.

"Who are you and where is she!" I yell. Alessandro walked towards me and snatched the phone from me.

"Tell me where my daughter is or I swear I WILL KILL THE SHIT OUT OF YOU!" He says, losing it.

"Oh, miss her already? You know what you have to do if you want your daughter back. Bring me Amalia and you'll get your daughter back." With that, the man ended the call.

His voice tho, sounded familiar.

Alessandro briefly glared at me and then his eyes softened. "What are we going to do?" He asks.

"There is nothing we can do." I start. "I will go to them and get Lily back." I add.

"There is no way you are doing that!" Demetrio disapprove and Alessandro shook his head as a no.

"Yes! She will! She is the reason my daughter has been kidnapped!" Amanda yells, attacking me. Alessandro held her back.

"Enough!" He yells.

"I will go and no one will stop me!" I firmly say and hopped in the car. I locked the door before anyone could stop me and started the engine.

Alessandro stood in front of the car and didn't move. I yelled at him to move, but he didn't budge. He stood there like a statue, not letting me drive. I got mad and got out of the car.

"Let me go!"

"You are not going, Amalia! We need to plan before doing anything." He replies.

"How could you be this cold! Our daughter is kidnapped!" Amanda yells. "It is all your fault, Amalia!" She adds.

"Enough!" Demetrio yells. "Everyone, get into the car, we are going home."

———

ALESSANDRO

I didn't think that it will arrive to this. I never thought that they would kidnap my daughter. I should have thought about it, but maybe because she was with her mother and no one knew about her, that I thought nothing would happen. They must have seen Lily at Amalia's house. Someone was indeed watching and if not, there is someone on the inside who is working with the other side.

"Alessandro..." a voice calls. I turn my face and see Amalia standing by the doorway.

She walks towards me and sits beside me. Putting her hand on top of mine, she says, "I am sorry." She says, sadly.

"Why are you apologizing? It is not your fault." I try to say, but she immediately shook her head.

"It is. Lily was kidnapped because of me and I am scared. I don't want anything to happen to her." She explains.

"Mo one is going to hurt her and we are going to safe her, don't worry." I reply, hugging her.

She had this concerned look on her face. Also, she had an expression that I couldn't decipher. I wanted to calm her down, but I couldn't. All I could think about is my Lily and the fact if I will continue with this work after finding her or not. I know that I cannot leave Amalia alone; she is the love of my life, but Lily...I couldn't put her through that again.

At midnight, Amalia received a message of a location from an unknown number. Demetrio, Amalia, River, Mia, and I went to the basement to get ready for the mission of saving Lily.

"Okay, this is mot the first mission that we do, but listen carefully." Demetrio starts, as he takes out the map of the location he printed out.

"I will have ten men come from this side and we are going to come from this side—since we still don't know who is behind this, we have to be careful. Do not act without me telling you. Don't do something stupid."

I rolled my eyes at what he said. He was too bossy.

"Amalia, who do you think is behind this?" Mia asks.

"I don't know, but I am sure that it is someone from the circle." She replies.

"How are you so sure?"

"I had a partner called Jeremy Stone. Before he died, he told me that some people in the circle are conspiring against me. Before he died, he was going to meet me and probably tell me who, but he was killed. Someone killed him for the information." She explains.

"I wonder why do they want you dead?" River mumbles.

"I wish to know. All I could think about is because of power, but I don't think that's all." She says.

"Do you have something that they want? Something other than power...something materialistic." Demetrio suggests.

"I have many things, Demetrio." She replies cockily.

I love that side of her.

"Fine." He rolls his eyes.

"Look, the best idea is to give myself in and you get Lily out." She tries again.

"That's never going to happen." I say firmly.

"I got nothing to lose, but you have."

"I will not lose you, Amalia." I groan. I grab the guns I am going to use on the mission and put them on each side of my jeans. I wore a bulletproof vest and gave one to Amalia.

"Alessandro..." Amalia calls.

"Yes?"

"Whatever happens, know that I love you, okay?" She whispers, sadly.

I smile and say, "I love you too, my Amalia."

——————

Hey guys! Here is a new chapter! I know I have taken too long to update, but I finally did! I tried to finish this chapter today and post it.

Just want to say some things! You are going to hate one or more characters in the upcoming chapters, but that do NOT mean that they are bad! It is just a situation that's going to happen

Also, what are your thoughts on the next chapters???

Thanks again for waiting and for keeping up with me

Word count: 1724

# 18. Saving Lily

AMALIA

Do people sense before they die, that they are going to die? It was something that I had always wondered. I never thought that the day of my death was this close. I thought that I'd live longer, but I would do anything for Lily.

We were on our way to the location they sent to my phone. I knew that something bad could happen, so I made sure I had a back-up plan. A plan that no one knew about, but me. I wouldn't tell anyone about it because I know they wouldn't agree. I might be selfish, but I cannot live knowing that I was the reason one of them died.

"Amalia, don't leave Alessandro's side." Demetrio says, while loading his gun. I nodded in response. I was afraid that if I opened my mouth and spoke, I would tell them my plan, so I stayed quiet.

The driver stopped the car, parking it somewhere hidden. They knew we were coming, but they didn't know when. However, it was clear that we weren't going to wait even if the sun was still up.

We stepped out of the Tahu and slowly walked to our positions. The building they were staying in had only two entrances . One from the front and one through the tunnels. We hoped that they didn't know that this building had tunnels. All of us stayed together beside Demetrio, who went with his men through the front door. The rest of us, walked towards the cellar that was linked to the tunnels.

"Don't leave my side." Alessandro whispered, kissing the top of my head. I knew he wasn't okay, hell no one would be when their daughter is kidnapped by killers. But he tried to stay with me and never left my side. What did I do to deserve a man like that? Why did I even chose him to work for me?

We entered the cellar and the smell was disgusting. The tunnels smelled awful as if a body was stashed somewhere here. We slowly walked, making our way to the entrance of the building. Rats walked beside us and honestly, they looked cute. Don't come for me.

I was holding my gun tightly. I knew how to fight, I am not that helpless, but I couldn't do it alone. That's one reason why I needed a bodyguard. We kept walking until we heard footsteps, so we stopped as River halted us with his fist like the military soldiers. We quickly his on the sides of the walls, waiting for the person to come. Once the footsteps were close, Alessandro and River quickly knocked him out with their guns. After making sure he was out cold, Alessandro took my hand and we started walking again. I wanted to tell him that I could walk on my own, but I wanted to savor this moment while it lasts.

Arriving at the end of the tunnel, we saw a door. It was locked, but Mia managed to open it, as she was skilled with this type of things. She slowly opened the door and peeked inside. Once she made sure that the way is clear, she opened it further and we stepped inside. As we were walking we heard gunshot. It must be Demetrio and the men. We quickly made our way to the sound and we saw a war going on. Demetrio told us not to engage because he was buying us time to find Lily, so we quickly walked the other way and began searching for her. We searched few rooms on this floor, but we didn't find anything. I was afraid that they would have done something to her because we already killed a lot of their men.

Suddenly, a man emerged shooting us. We quickly ducked and began shooting back. The man was good. He shot us again, as one of his bullets grazed my shoulder. I hissed at the feeling. Alessandro's face hardened and he stood up and ran to the man in a suicide mission and shot him before he could. I was so mad at him for going openly like that, but it warmed my heart to see him defend and protect me.

"Thank you." I murmured, giving him a kiss. I hope their plan works because if it didn't, I don't know what will happen next.

We entered an elevator and pressed the too floor, which is where they are probably keeping Lily. Now going into an elevator is not the best plan we came up with because we don't know what is on the other side of the door when it opens. How many men will they be?

Upon reaching the top floor, the door opened revealing five me. As if on instinct, River and Mia shot two, Alessandro shot the one on his left, and I surprisingly shot the on to my right. There was one left that River shot after that.

"She should be somewhere here." I said, marching towards each door and checking in.

"Stay by my side." Sandro groans.

I opened the last door on this floor and there she was, sitting on a chair, with her hands cuffed, and a duck tape around her pretty mouth. When she saw us, her eyes widen and she started crying.

How could they treat a child this way? How could they tape her mouth and chain her to the chair? Don't they have mercy for the child? She is harmless.

"Baby!" Alessandro ran to his daughter, trying to free her from the uncomfortable chair, but before he could do that, a group of men came through the door, surrounding us. We didn't shoot because not only was Lily here, but also we were outnumbered. I glanced at the middle and I couldn't believe my eyes.

"Cintinio?" I say, as I looked at the man in front of me. He was the new guy in the circle. Was he on this from the beginning or?

"Amalia Ferrari." My name rolled out of his mouth, making my insides fill with unease.

"Why are you doing this!" I ask, angrily.

"Answer her, you—!" Alessandro yells, not completing his sentence. He didn't want to swear in front of his daughter or scare her more than she was scared.

"As you can see, you are outnumbered." Cintinio started and I knew where this is going. I was just scared of one thing, what if he killed them all?

"If you want to save the girl, you know what you should do." He glanced my way. His eyes said it all.

I walked towards Lily and removed the tape. I then un-cuffed her, as she stood up and hugged me. She the. Hugged her father and stayed in his arm.

"I knew you would come, daddy!" She cries, making my heart clench. It all happened because of me and Cintinio seemed to sense what I was thinking because of what he said next, "Yes, Amalia. It is."

He was referring to what happened. It was indeed my fault.

"What do you want?" Alessandro groans, holding his daughter tightly.

"I believe Amalia knows what I want." He replies, smugly.

I sure as hell knew what he wanted.

•FLASHBACK•

"I am glad you decided to talk, Sara." I say to the 15 year old girl.

"I have to tell you something." She starts, as she turns around to check if her mother came home or not.

"Before my dad died, I heard him say something about a code to something very important. When I walked into his office the next day, I found him dead. I checked his desk and found this paper." She hands me the paper. I glance at it and found a code that was not deciphered.

"What is this?" I ask, confused.

"I don't know, but his book might tell you something." She adds, handing my a small journal.

"Thank you, Sara."

"Please, don't come here again and don't tell mother. She told me not to trust anyone, but I somehow...trust you." She says and I nod.

I admired this young brave girl. She was just fifteen years old and was brave enough to call me again and talk to me.

•END OF FLASHBACK•

Well, that secret code? It turned out to be a code that helps you hack the government's documents of the Nuclear weapons. Where they were stored, will they be used, how they were done, etc. Now as much as I hated the government, I couldn't hand it to a criminal. I don't even know how Jeremy Stone found this code. I deciphered it alright, but I threw the code at the same time, but I never forgot the numbers, just in case.

"What does he want, Amalia?" River asks this time.

"Give me the code, Amalia." Cintinio sings, waving with his gun.

"Fine. I'll give it to you once you let them all leave safely." I lied smoothly.

"No!" Alessandro yells, but I just ignored him. As much as I loved him, I couldn't put him and his daughter in danger.

"Leave." I yell at them.

"We are not going to leave." Mia says, frowning.

I didn't know what to do. I had an idea but I didn't want to do it in front of Lily, so I motioned for Alessandro to cover her eyes.

"Leave or I do this." I aim the gun to my head. "I'll die with my secret and he will kill you." I got my manipulating skills back and weirdly, it felt good.

"Amalia!" Alessandro yells, a tear rolled down his face, as he held his daughter tightly.

"Didn't see that coming." Cintinio chuckles, as if the scene before him was the most interesting he had ever seen.

"Please, leave." My voice cracks. I tried my best not to shed a tear because I will never ever cry in front of my enemies.

I glanced at River, giving him a look of "take them out and leave" and he understood. He took Mia and grabbed Alessandro's arm; which he struggled with, and walked out of the room. Alessandro's yells filled the room, as my heart clench because of what I did. Just few hours ago, he told me that he wasn't going to lose me, when I knew he will. I knew everything here was going to happen, that's why I made a plan b.

"So, where were we?" Cintinio starts.

"I am not going to say anything until I see them leave." I say, firmly.

"You are not going to talk at all, aren't you?" He chuckles, knowing that I was not going to open my mouth and tell him the code.

"I knew that—but you are here, aren't you? We have all the time we need." He smirks, making his way towards me.

———

I hope you liked this chapter you guys!!! What fo you think of it? I tried to come up with something, a reason as to why Cintinio wants her (which will not be the only reason ;), so I came up with this. Also,

I didn't want Jeremy Stone to die without at least giving something. That's the least he could do!

Thank you guys for being patient with me and I will try to update tomorrow as well! Finger-crossed

Don't forget to comment and vote

Word count: 1900

# 19. Secrets

AMALIA

Tied into the chair, I received another slap across my face. "Tell me! What is it?" Cintinio barked.

I had been here for 15 hours and I haven't said a word, yet. He'd be stupid if he thought that I would tell him the code.

"Pathetic." He spat, as he chuckled. He was about to say something when I cut him off.

"Answer my question, then I'll think about answering you."

"And what is your question?"

"Who are you and how do you know me." I ask. How did he even know that I have the code? Could Angelina; Jeremy's wife, found out that Sara gave me the code and told him? Because I know he wouldn't leave her alone because of the code. He seemed to do anything for the code. He was desperate.

"You are really pathetic that you don't remember me." He laughs. I looked intently at him, but I had no memory of him. I don't know this person. Who the fuck is he?

"My brother came to work for you and get information, but later died because he was about to open his mouth." He reveals, shocking me.

"You're?—"

"Franco; Gino's brother? Yes."

I looked at him, remembering Gino's older brother, who him and I never got along because he hated my guts. What happened to this family?

Then it struck me . . . Did Franco kill his own brother because he was about to confess to Demetrio? If yes, how?

"What did you do to Gino?" The question rolls out of my mouth, as my lips parted.

He chuckles. "I should have killed him a long time ago, but now he is finally dead."

I was lost for words. How could someone kill his own sibling?

"Why?" I find myself asking.

He walks around me as he 'tskd' trying to intimidate me. "You ask a lot of question, cugino." He says, dangerously.

"Why did you kill him?" I yell this time. I wanted to know if my theory was right.

His face hardens. "The thing about Gino is that he has a soft spot for you, but that didn't stop him from trying to take you down." He smirks. "I killed him because he was about to confess to that mafia boss of yours because he felt regret, and I don't do regrets."

He was talking as if he wasn't talking about his own brother. I remember when Gino used to tell me how much his brother is a good man even if he didn't like me, but I didn't believe him. He told me how he used to protect him against the bullies at school. So what happened to Franco that he had to kill his own brother? It had to be about this plan. The plan to kidnap Lily to lure me in.

"You are a monster!" I yell, trying to control my anger so that I don't cry. I do tend to cry when I am very angry.

"So were your parents, cugino." He spat, his voice laced with venom.

What did he mean by that? What had my parents done?

"What do you mean?" I ask, still confused of what he had meant.

"Why do you think your parents died, Amalia?"

Wait a second . . .

He killed my parents? H-he

"You!" I bark, trying to get free from these ropes.

"Your dear father was in the mafia with mine, but because of that mother of yours, he decided to leave. My father had agreed, but he didn't know that your fucking father would tell the authorities. That's why we had to fly and leave the country!" He explains, his voice was laced with anger, sadness, and an emotion I couldn't decipher.

"But my father was arrested before we all could leave. And because of that, I didn't leave with Gino and mother, I came back to town and killed your fucking traitor parents." He spat the last part.

I couldn't believe what I was hearing. The man in front of me; my cousin, killed me parents? The man that I have been searching for was standing here and I couldn't do anything about it.

"You are sick." That was the only thing that I could say.

"Yes, I am, and that's because of your family!" He yells, walking towards me. He took a hold of my shoulders tightly, forcing me to look into his scary dark eyes.

"I will kill Alessandro and his daughter, so you could feel the pain I felt. It's unfortunate that Annie is dead, I would have loved to have killed her."

"If you touch one hair of any of them, I swear to god, Franco, I will bury you alive." I say, dangerously, as he scoffs not believing me.

I was about to say something when he beats me to it. "Now, let's talk about the future my favorite cugino." He strokes my left cheek and I wanted to vomit.

"You will tell me the code because if you didn't, you know what will happen." He says.

I wanted to anger him for some reason, so I did what I do best, be a bitch. "Oh, really?" I rise my eyebrows, as I fake a surprised reaction. "What will happen? I don't recall you mentioning anything about that." I act stupid.

He takes a hold of my hair tightly and leans closer to me. "You might think you are smart, but you are not."

"I wouldn't really believe that from a stupid person." I frown, biting my bottom lips so I don't laugh.

Anger was evident on his face as he couldn't control it any longer. A sound echoed in the room as he slapped me. Another slap echoed on the other side of my cheek. All along, I was only laughing because trust me, it was funny.

"Why are you laughing?" He yells, hitting me one more time.

"It's funny." I keep on laughing.

"What is funny? Tell me!"

"It's funny that you thought by giving me few slaps that you'll get the code or some sort of reaction—because let me tell you something, Franco, even if you kill me or anyone I love, you will not get that code and it will die with me. I am the only one who knows it." My serious voice took him off-guard.

It was true. I wasn't going to hand him the code even if he threatens to kill Alessandro and Lily. Don't think that I am heartless, but imagine Franco getting the code and using the nuclear weapons, how many people would die? The world would be in chaos. It didn't matter anymore because Alessandro and I are going on our separate ways, even if he doesn't know that now.

I will not put him in danger any longer.

* * *

ALESSANDRO

I kept rocking back and forth, trying to calm my traumatized daughter down. I cannot imagine what she had gone through. He is still five years old and I cannot believe that she has to endure all of this at such a young age.

Amalia on the other hand did not leave my mind. Every second she occupies my mind, leaving me wondering what the hell is happening to her. I still cannot wrap my head around what had happened. How could she turn herself in without telling me. When she told me yesterday; before we left for the mission, that she loves me no matter what happened, I didn't dwell on it that much, but now I know what she meant. She was saying goodbye, as if she knew our plan would not work. As much as I am grateful for her for saving my daughter, I didn't want her to turn herself in. I could have saved them both. I know I could.

"Did you find out anything about the code?" Demetrio suddenly asks, cutting off my thoughts.

"I haven't searched, yet. Amalia didn't even tell me about the code or that it existed." I say in disbelief. Didn't she trust me enough to tell me? But then again, it is better for only one person to know information like this.

"Father, we found something." Mia comes into the office with River trailing behind her. I really admire those two. They are inseparable. I hope Amalia and I be like that in the future. I know we have a very strong relationship that is not going to break no matter what, but I want to be closer to her, emotionally and mentally. I want to be beside her 24/7. I love her so much that I want to go back there right now and get her back, but I cannot leave Lily in this state. She hasn't spoken since we returned and I was starting to get worried.

"What?" Demetrio asks.

"Few months ago, the government's nuclear program code was stolen by someone from the government. They haven't found him yet, but I did some digging and found who the person was. His name is Roberto Brambilla and he was seen few months ago with Jeremy Stone; Amalia's closest person in the circle or later was murdered." Mia explains as she gave us pictures of Jeremy Stone and Roberto Brambilla.

"So, Roberto gave the code to Jeremy?" I ask, trying to make sense of my theory.

"—and Jeremy gave it to Amalia before he died." Demetrio adds.

"Exactly! Which means, Cintinio wanted Amalia in the first place because he wanted the code. He knew she had the code because she was the closest to Jeremy." Mia says.

"So, what should we do now? We have to save her." I say quickly.

"Find more information about this...Cintinio. Any family member or someone he cares about." Demetrio orders River.

River huffs.

"What?" Mia and Demetrio snap at him.

"No offense, Alessandro, but Mia and ai have been waiting to go on this date." For some reason, I smile because I know he was joking and just wanted to change the atmosphere.

"Go find me information before I kill you." Demetrio growls. River's face paled, as he ran outside the office. Mia broke out laughing and so did Demetrio.

"I wish I didn't hire him in the first place, all of this wouldn't have happened." He mutters, earning a glare from his daughter.

"Alessandro, I would like to talk to you about a matter." Demetrio starts, signaling for his daughter to leave.

"Yes, Demetrio?"

"I was thinking about you and Lily and I think it's best if you leave the country." He says, firmly. I didn't why he was saying something like that when he knows that I will never leave Amalia, especially not before making sure she's safe.

"I will not leave Amalia." I voice my thoughts.

"I will save her, I promise, but you are not safe here."

* * *

Hey guys! I hope you like this chapter! I know I said that I'll update yesterday, but I really didn't have time, sorry.

Anyways, what are your thoughts on this chapter? Did you figure that Franco/Cintinio is Gino's brother? He changed his name so Amalia wouldn't know him, even though, she didn't really recognize him.

Word count: 1866

# 20. Good-bye

This chapter has multiple POVs—sorry for that. ***

AMALIA

The sound of my spit echoed in the room. My mouth was full of my own blood, so I had to spit it out. He had been punching me for few minutes that I eventually broke out laughing. I kept on laughing and he kept on punching, thinking that I'll give in and tell him to stop. I'd never do that. He mustn't know me well if he thought that I'll give in.

Another one.

I laugh out loud.

"Why are you laughing!" He yells, getting extremely frustrated. He doesn't like to lose and he clearly loves to see people in pain. It's just happens that I am one of the people who doesn't show that I am in pain. Thank goodness, I was able to bring the old Amalia back. It's like the vampire switch that they do to turn off their humanity, but in my case, I turn . . . Oh it's the same thing.

I don't answer him and he gets more furious. "I said, answer me!" He yells, blessing me with another slap. This time, I laugh hard.

A look of disbelief passes through his face as he turns around and leaves the room. One thing I learned is that when you don't give your kidnapper the reaction they want, they'll leave you alone.

Once he left, I quickly unmasked my emotions, as I groan in pain. It hurt like hell and it was all in the face. I spit more blood as they keep on coming in.

This is the first time I don't see something coming. Hell, it never really crossed my mind that he'll kidnap Lily ir that he is my cousin. Why didn't I think of that? I was too blinded by love. That's the only thing I could come up with. It didn't only endanger me, but also Alessandro and his daughter. I don't know what would I have done if something bad happened to Lily. I would have probably killed myself. I could never look Alessandro in the eye if something happened to her. That's why ai need him to leave. Leave far away with his daughter. He gains no good when he is around me. I am a messed up spoiled rich manipulating bitch. I do him no good.

* * *

ALESSANDRO

Fuck, yes.

We just got information about Cinintio and found that his father is still alive. He is hiding somewhere Italy and we just have to find out where. The only thing I came up with is to kidnap his father, make him call his son for a meeting with him and that he should bring

Amalia to speak with her since they are related, and then when he comes, we kill them both.

"But they are going to know if Andre was kidnapped." Mia argues, not liking my idea. Andre Valentino is Gino's and Franco/Cintinio's father.

"But we could kill everyone before they make a phone call." I argue back.

"What if Franco called them and they didn't answer? Surely he'll know."

"Then we make Andre call him right after w take him."

"And what should he tell him? What if Andre didn't even have a phone or something."

"Mia, you are making it so complicated." Demetrio says. "We could take one of the guard's phones." He adds.

"Yeah." I agree with him.

"Fine." She huffs, "but we need to find him first." She says, pacing back and forth.

I am about to say something when River cut me off by barging into the room. "That won't be necessary, I found him - he is staying in a small house North of Sicily in a city called Cefalù."

"What the fuck is he doing there?" I ask, confusedly.

"My guess is chilling. There are a lot of beaches there." Mia guesses.

"There are beaches all over Sicily." I roll my eyes, taking the papers from River. I glance at them, making sure to memorize the location.

"We leave now." I announce, earning confused looks.

"Now?" Demetrio frowns.

"Oh, you are right. Amalia can wait." I mock. My anger is starting to rise. How could he even suggest to wait? Why should we wait?

"I didn't mean it like it—what I mean is that we should gather more information." He tries to explain.

"We leave, now." I finalize, exiting the room. What information could we possibility gather more? We already know Andre's hiding and the only thing we need to do is go there and take him. Then we call his bastard of a son, and make a meeting. That's it.

* * *

We got ready to leave for our mission. Since we are in Florence, we have to leave now because it takes time to go back to Sicily.

"Are you ready?" I ask everyone and they nod.

We make our way to Demetrio's private jet and get seated. One advantage we have is that we have this private jet. I mean he has this private jet.

"Don't be reckless out there, understood?" Demetrio warns.

"Understood." I sigh, deeply.

For the next few hours, I was on my nerves, as I couldn't wait toll we reach Cefalù. My mind keeps drifting off to Amalia and what could she be doing now. Was she hurt? Is she being tortured? Is she . . . Dead?

She can't be.

"Calm down, you are making me nervous." River hisses.

"I can't—when Mia gets kidnapped, you will understand how I feel.."

"Actually, I know because Mia was kidnapped few years back, it sucks."

"Really?" I lift my eyebrow in surprise. I didn't know Mia was kidnapped. Hell, this family is weird, all of them got kidnapped. What the hell do they do?

"Trust me, Amalia is strong and she is okay." He tries to soothe me.

"Thanks, kid." I nod in gratitude.

After few hours, the plane landed. We unfasten our seatbelts and make our way out of the jet. The fresh air of Sicily hits my nose, as memories flood through me. Our time here was precious. It was the best days of my life...being with Amalia I mean.

We rent a car from the airport and drive to Cefalù. I have never been in the Northern part of Sicily, but from what I gathered, it is a quiet place, or at least of most it is quiet.

"Did you get the exact location?" Demetrio asks his daughter.

"From what I searched, it could only be in two places, so we will check them both." She replies, confidently.

Mia is a great kid. She is smart and strong. I haven't known her that much, but from my short time with her, she seems nice.

"Good." He says.

After some time, we arrive to the first location. It was an abandoned house close to the beach. There was no neighboring houses and the only thing close to it was the beach and a small mechanic shop.

We step out of the car, making sure to check our surroundings. I take out my gun from my holster and removed the safety pin just in case of a sudden attack. We walk together towards the house and till now there isn't any sign of anyone. When we reach the front door, we count to three and break the door down. From the looks of the outside where there wasn't any guards, there wasn't anyone here, but we had to make sure in case he is staying without guards, so he doesn't grab attention.

We split up and I go upstairs because that's where they mostly are. By they I mean the hiders. Checking every room, when I make sure there wasn't anyone, I go downstairs.

"Clear!" I say loudly.

"There isn't anyone here. He must be staying in the other location." Mia says, looking around.

"And is that other location far from here?" I ask.

"No, five minutes—let's go."

We hop into the car again and drive to the second and last potential location. My patience is growing weak, as I couldn't wait to see Amalia. I need to see her or else I would lose it.

Parking in a hidden location, we check around to find many guards surrounding a house. It was too obvious that there was someone very important inside. I couldn't help but smirk at what Andre's reaction might be when he finds that we are here for him. We step out of the car carefully, as I set up the silencer into my gun. I tell the rest to do the same because there were many guards and we needed to be as quiet as we could—for the first part at least.

Making our war towards the back of the house, I nod at Demetrio telling him that I will kill the two guards on my right. He is going to take the other two on his side. Mia and River are going to go from the front, so in that way, we killed everyone outside. With a simple nod from Demetrio, I fire my gun killing the two. We reach the back door and we hear the front door being pushed open. We do the same. There were at least 5 in the living room and so, we act fast. I kill the one to my right, as I search for more but they are all dead. Mia, River, and Demetrio took care of it. We hear voices upstairs and we make our way up. Climbing the stairs carefully, I spot two guards and a man. The man's eyes land on me and before he could react, I kill the the two guards, then aiming my gun at him.

"Do not move." I say, dangerously.

"Who the fuck are you!" He yells, backing away.

"You don't need to know who we are—what you need to know is that we are going to take you with us." Demetrio explains.

"Where?"

"Well, that little son of yours kidnapped someone we care about, so you are going to help us get her back." I smile, evilly.

"Because if you didn't, we will kill you, and we both know that you value your life more than your son's." Mia says.

She must know a lot of things about Andre to say that. Damn.

He nods vigorously, afraid we would do something to him. He walks with us to the car silently. We step into the car and drive off.

* * *

AMALIA

"We have been over this, I will not tell you the code." I sign, as he slaps me for the millionth time. My face must be red right now, covered in blood.

"Well, I figured that, so I am going to try something else." He smirks, evilly.

"And what is that? cut my fingers?" I smile, smugly.

"That's a great idea, but no—how about we talk about how I killed your parents?" He smiles, whipping the smile on my face.

This is not happening.

"You know, as I told you before, after my father was arrested; which I later got him out, I returned to your parents house—" He smirks, "—do you want to know what happened next?" He taunts.

I shake my head.

"—I went in, shot your mother in the head and then shot your father in the heart." He laughs at my reaction.

"I then burned the house down." He concludes the story.

"Do you want me to repeat it?" He taunts again, getting close to me as I shake my head vigorously.

"Stop."

"I killed your mother in the head—"

"STOP!" I yell, trying to break free from the ropes. His laugh echoed in the room, finding pleasure in destroying me mentally and emotionally. But what he doesn't know is that I can fucking mask my pain even if I had lost my act few seconds ago.

He looks me in the eyes and says, "now tell me, where is the code." His face hardens.

"Did you think that I was affected by this story?" I smirk, when I was dying from the inside.

"Huh?"

"My mommy and daddy died a long time ago and right now, I don't give two shits." I say in a child's voice.

I am sorry

"You are crazy." He frowns, as he stands up. He couldn't believe what he is hearing.

"I know." I shrug.

I am about to say something when his phone rings. He takes his phone out of his pocket whilst looking at me.

"Yes?"

"Father?"

"Where are you!"

"I am coming." He says and is about to leave, when he looks back at me.

"Why?"

"Okay." He hung up.

"We are leaving." He declares, motioning for his men to untie me. He must be taking me to his father because he seemed to be talking to him on the phone. I didn't know that his father was still alive. I though he died in prison or something.

One of his men unties me, grabs my arm harshly, and walk outside with me trailing behind. He ties my hands, leaving my legs free to walk. He pushes me into the car and Franco follows, sitting beside me.

"Where are we going?" I ask.

He looks at me, rolling his eyes. "Your uncle wants to see you, haven't you missed him?" He smirks.

"I sure did." I answer, honestly. I did miss uncle Andre . . . well that's before I knew that his son killed my parents.

"Does your father know that you killed Gino?" I ask, waiting patiently for his answer.

"The idea was his." He says, shocking me.

I definitely don't miss him. If he killed his son, what would he do to me?

After few minutes on the road, we arrive. He pulls my arm, taking me out of the car, roughly. We walk inside the building, into the living room. There he stood; my uncle, in the middle, holding a cup of whiskey. He turns around our way and smiles, but I could sense that he is not okay.

"My dear, Amalia. You have grown up." He says, placing the cup on the table.

"Uncle." I nod.

"Why did you call me here? and why did you leave your house." Franco demands, as he walks towards his father. He is about to respond when another voice cut him off. A voice I didn't think I'd hear again.

"Because we forced him to." Alessandro replies, aiming his gun at Franco. Mia, River, and Demetrio were here as well and they were aiming at the rest of the guards. Mia walks my way; still aiming at the guards, and grabs my hand gently, as she walks back to them. Suddenly, we hear gunshots. Demetrio and River killed the guards. It was only us, Franco, and Erik.

"How could you do that?" Franco growls at his father.

"What could you expect from a father who killed his own son?" I voice my thoughts. Mia unties me, freeing my hands.

"I am sorry, son. They were going to kill me." A tear slips from Andre's eyes. I cannot believe that he is capable of crying.

"It's over, Franco." Alessandro declares, as he hand-cuffs him. River does the same with Erik.

"What are you going to do?" Franco asks.

"We are going to hand you to the authorities." Demetrio replies.

"Why not kill us?" He asks, again.

"Death is too good for you." I say this time.

* * *

We are back in Florence. We have handed my cousin and uncle to the authorities. I still cannot believe that I am back and that I finally know who killed my parents. It's too sad that Annie isn't alive to hear the truth. A part of me always knew that Annie knew who did it, but I refuse to believe it. She couldn't do that to me.

"Amalia?" Alessandro's voice said. My heart is beating so fast. I turn around and look at him. He looked so tired.

"I missed you." His voice breaks, pulling me into a hug. I hug him back. I have missed him so much.

"Me too."

He breaks the hug and smashes his lips onto mine. Once again, as if it is the first time, butterflies flew everywhere in my body.

"Don't ever do that again." He says, hinting to when I turned myself in to Franco. I back away from him, as a tear slips onto my cheek. What I am about to do is going to destroy us both, but I couldn't let him stay with me when I know that I haven't been good to his or Lily's life. I still don't know if there are enemies after me. The circle is still there and some might complete when Franco started.

"Alessandro." I let go of his hand. A frown appears on his face.

"You should leave."

"What?" He chuckles, thinking that I am joking. His face hardens when he sees my serious one.

"You c-can't be serious, right?"

"I am." My voice breaks. "They kidnapped Lily because of me, can't you see that? And they might do it again."

"I can protect her—both of you. Amalia, pleas—"

"No, Alessandro. I cannot forgive myself if something happened to you both. I am not meant to fall in love, Alessandro. I don't deserve it." I am crying by now.

"Don't say that, please." His voice cracks, holding my hands tightly.

"I am sorry, good-bye, Alessandro."

With that, I turn around and leave for good.

* * *

Hey!!!

I hope you guys liked this chapter! It is a long one just like old times. I just want to point out something—I am sorry if my tenses are all of the place in the past few chapters, I am trying to get them right.

So, what do you think is going to happen in the next chapter? Will Amalia go back to Alessandro?

Don't forget to vote, comment, and share! it really means a lot <3

Word Count: 3000

# 21. Reunion

AMALIA

I wake up the next day feeling a little bit better than before. I do 't know if I'll ever recover from whatever happened a month ago, but hopefully, I will. The fact that he is not around me 24/7 like he used to, is just disturbing. I haven't seen him in exactly 30 days and I am going insane. I don't know if I will ever be okay without him around. I don't think I will.

I walk down the stairs after getting ready for my day. I have returned to my home and maximized my bodyguards. I couldn't hire another personal bodyguard because I felt it isn't right. I always wonder what he is doing. What his daughter is doing. Is he okay?

Demetrio told me if I wanted to know about Alessandro since he can get me information, but I told him no. I don't want to know anything and I don't want ti be in his life. I am nothing but a magnet to catastrophes.

I was about to call Annie when I remembered that she isn't here. She's dead. Great.

I entered the kitchen and found Ezekiel cooking breakfast. "What's for breakfast today?" I ask, coldly.

"Omelets." He hesitantly replies. I just nod.

I left to the living room, not being able to continue my tour around the house to check up on everything. I see Isabella standing, waiting for me.

"Good morning, Ms. Ferrari." She brightly greets.

When the attack happened on the house, Annie had told her to take a holiday from work. So, when I came back, I called her and told her to come.

"Good morning." I reply, lazily.

"Are we leaving to the company?" She asks.

"Yes, but first give me a summary of everything happened."

She starts explaining to me everything that had happened that past few months, when I was too busy to even think about my company. Thanks to Isabella, she had handled everything professionally. She didn't even need me. She was the best at her work and I don't regret hiring her.

"Okay, good." I reply, after she finished giving the summary. "Let's go."

We leave the house together and get into the Black Bentley. Three men accompanied us, one in the driver's, one in the passenger, and one at the back seat with us. I haven't had a problem so far with anything. The rest of the circle did not do anything and I actually quitted. I don't think I should be somewhere where everyone wants to kill me for a reason that I don't know about. I could understand why Franco wanted to kill me...you know because of the codes, but why did the rest wanted to? Maybe they wanted me to leave the circle and them handle everything. Maybe they get threatened from my wealth and all that, but again, they are wealthy.

But you are wealthier.

We arrive at the company safe and sound. I enter my office, while Isabella enters hers. Every since Alessandro left, or rather ever since I kicked him, I have been coming to the company. It is the only way to keep my mind off somethings.

I am working on my computer, when my office phone rings.

"Yes, Isabella?"

"Okay, let him in."

She called to let me know that the IT manager wants to talk to me. I hear a knock and I let him in.

"Ms. Ferrari." He greets with a nod.

"What is it?" I ask, coldly. You could say that I am only a little friendly with Isabella. No one else.

"We have fixed the network like you asked, but we still didn't do the website of the company."

"Why haven't you done that too?" I ask, harshly. I want everything to be perfect in my company.

"I-It didn't work like you wanted to, so we are redoing it again."

"Do it today and not tomorrow—do not leave until you finish." I command, earning a quick nod. He turns around and leaves, but not before I mutter some profanities. I hate when they do not do their jobs like they are required to. I did ask the whole IT department to finish the network connections and our website, since they weren't working, but they only do what they want to do. I have to change that. It seems that they are out if their game because I haven't been much in the company and I couldn't blame them because it is the truth.

I sit back on the chair and continue my work. Every now and then, I think of Annie, but I quickly try to brush it off and focus on something else. Also, sometimes I think if Alessandro, but again, I try to focus on something else. I just lost two of the most important people in my life—well, scratch that, three including Lily. I am all alone right not and I am all to blame.

After I finish everything, I call Isabella and I went home. I drove her to her house and then went to mine.

Once I walk into my house, I feel familiarity. I feel a little safe. I walk to my room and change my clothes and removing my makeup. The worst thing I hate is removing my makeup. I just...it is really tiring and it sucks, especially the mascara. I go under the covers, when Gus joins me. I miss him so much and it pains me a lot that I am not giving him much attention like before. I should focus on him more often.

* * * "Ms. Ferrari, there is someone by the door, who wishes to speak to you." Ashelia says. I just woke up and I went downstairs for breakfast.

"Who is it?" I ask, when he face falls. I suddenly know who it is. Rebecca.

"Let her in." I say before she says anything else. Before Annie died, everything she had wanted was to get my sister and I back together. I am not saying that I will, but the least that I could do is honor Annie's wishes in some way.

"Amalia..." Rebecca gives me a weak smile, not believing that I let her in. She looks good, not bad, but dark circles cover her under eyes. She looks skinnier than before, as if she is not eating at all. She looks tired in general.

"Rebecca." I nod, motioning for her to sit, which surprised her. She takes a seat carefully, trying to let her nerves calm. She wasn't like this, you know. She was arrogant, self-centered, egoistic, and a total bitch. She was too confident for her own good—not that being confident is not good, but she was a lot to the point that she thought that she was always right.

"I heard about Annie." She swallows, hardly. "I wanted to come earlier, but I was scared you wouldn't want to see me." She adds.

"It's good you didn't." I nod in approval. If she did come before, I would have literally killed her.

"I am sorry, Amy." My breath hitches at the nickname she gave me. She hasn't called me Amy in a long time. It reminds me of the good times when we were teenagers.

"I am sorry for everything—for what I did in the past, I am sorry I betrayed you. I am sorry I stood in Castelo's side and not yours—I am sorry I didn't believe you and sorry that I cheated and betrayed you." She sobs.

"I am a terrible person and I know that, but you are my sister, please forgive me."

My eyes prickle, as I feel tears are about to run down. I try to stop them, but it did not work. Soon enough, they run down onto my cheeks.

"I forgive you." I say the words I have never thought I would say. I keep saying that I am doing this for Annie, but deep down, I have forgiven her along time ago.

She is taken aback from my confession. Her brows furrow and a confused expression cover her face. But a small smile comes to surface once she understood what I said. She stands up quickly and runs to me for a hug. She hugs me tightly, as if her life depends on me. I hesitantly hug her back.

"Thank you." Her voice breaks. She is too emotional.

"I am sorry." I say out of the blue. She pulls back and looks at me confusedly.

"Sorry that I treated you like rubbish." I clarify.

"I deserved it, all of it." She tries to make me feel good, but it doesn't work.

"No, you didn't." I reply. "You didn't deserve it all."

* * *

Hey guys! I hope you are doing well. I hope you liked this a little short chapter (sorry for that) but I didn't want to focus in anything else other than Amalia and Rebecca! Finally we could say we have a new permanent character.

Also, what do you think Alessandro is doing? Is he moving on or...?

Do 't forget to vote, comment, and share!

Word count: 1530

# 22. "Why Did You Leave Me."

AMALIA

The summer weather of Sicily is the best. I absolutely love this weather, it makes my skin warm and cozy. I am currently walking with Rebecca along the beach, for a fresh air. We have been talking for the past week about our lives and tried to get past of what happened. I know I said I would never forgive her, but truth be told, I have missed her. I will always love my sister no matter what.

"Aren't you going to talk to him?" She asks, referring to Sandro. I had told her about him and about everything that happened. I had no one else to talk to and she was there for me and still is.

"No, I could never." I reply, weakly. As much as I want to pick up my phone and call him, I know I couldn't and shouldn't. The last thing I need is him coming to my house with Lily and suddenly an attack happens. I don't want to put him or Lily in danger, especially when I still am not sure if someone is after me or not. There probably is.

"Rebecca...I have to tell you something." I start. One thing I didn't mention the past week when we were talking was how our parents died. I couldn't tell her back then, but I guess I am ready now. She has the right to know.

"What?" She asks, confused.

"There is something I haven't told you, yet—about our parents." I say, making her frown. "They were murdered, but I haven't told you who killed then." I sigh. "It was Uncle Andre and his kids."

"What?!"

Rebecca was a year younger than me, which makes her 14 when our parents died. When I was with my ex, Rebecca was with me too, until I moved to London for a while.

"I can't believe it." She swallows hard. "Amalia, I have to tell you something." She nervously said.

"What is it?"

"I think Gino knew your location because of me."

"You gave it to him?!"

"I didn't know he wanted to kill you." A tear escapes her eye.

"It's fine. It's over now." I say and continue walking.

* * *

Rebecca and I walked back home. It was days like this that I hate. Days where I don't have anything to do. I know I have a job, but when you are the boss, you can do whatever you want. I tried to drown myself with work, but it didn't work out. The thought of Alessandro are not leaving my mind. I keep wondering what he's doing.

A phone ring pull me out of my thoughts. I look on the screen to find an unknown number. This better not be a killer or something.

"Hello?" I say once I pick up. No one talks on the other line. "Hello?" I say again.

"Nanny Amalia?" Lily's cute voice says.

"Lily? Is that you?" I ask. How did she get my number? Or more importantly, from what phone is she calling from.

"It's me." She says. "Why did you leave me?" Her voice cracks making my heart clench.

The thing is, my lawyer finally won the case against Lily's mother m, Amanda. Lily was in Alessandro's custody now. If it wasn't like that, I would have left her. I would have done anything to get Alessandro the custody. But again, I know what she meant.

"Baby..." I didn't know what to say.

"I miss you. Come, please." She pleads. Tears threatened to fall, but I control them.

"Is your dad around?" I ask, ignoring her previous statement.

"No. He is sleeping—I am sitting with a nanny that I hate. She is not you and not good." She says.

"Oh, why do you hate hate her?" I ask, amused.

"I told you, she is not you—besides, she yells at me." As soon as she says that, my blood boils. How could she yell at her?

"Did you tell your father?"

"No. I don't want to upset him." I could feel her pout.

"Tell him, Lily. He will get upset if you didn't." I try to convince her.

"Are you sure?"

"Yes, I am sure, baby."

She is about to say something, when Alessandro calls her. "Lily? Whoa re you talking to?"

I am about to tell her don't say who, when she says, "Amalia, daddy."

"Amalia?" Alessandro's voice says through the phone. He must have snatched the phone from his daughter.

"Amalia...please, answer me." He pleads.

But I didn't. I hung up. I couldn't. I couldn't talk to him because I know that if I did, I will tell him to come and I couldn't afford that now. He needs to be safe and that's all that matters.

* * *

The next day arrived and I got ready for the day. I had to go to my company and do the daily check-ups. I know Isabella is there, but I have to make sure of everything. As much as she is smart and hardworking, everyone is bound to make mistakes and I cannot afford that now.

I wear my white dress-shirt, pairing it up with white heels, and leave my room. Walking downstairs, I hear footsteps coming from behind. Looking back, I see Rebecca.

"Good morning." I say.

"Good morning, sister." She replies with a smile.

An idea suddenly comes to me. Rebecca is not working and I think that a giving her a job will help her stand up and be dependent on herself. I know that she wants to work, but is afraid or embarrassed to ask me even though we are sisters. But I know it is not easy for her since we have been away from each other for a long time. I want to help her become responsible, especially if something bad happening to me. Trust me, as much as I love my sister, I don't trust her with my wealth. My wealth is going straight to Lily. Shocking, I know. I decided that Lily is going to inherit my wealth; all of it.

"Rebecca?"

"Yes?" She replies, as she sits on the chair to eat breakfast.

"I have been meaning to ask you, do you want to work?"

"Umm, I actually would love you." A smile broke on her face.

"Great, then you will come with me today to the company." I say with a proud smile. She nods.

I just couldn't believe how fast our relationship moved. Within a month, we were back to Amy and Becca; the inseparable sisters. As much as I hated her for a while, I had many reasons and I had the right. But now getting back to her and removing those walls that were around me, I really see what I missed on, even when she betrayed my trust. She is still my sister and I can see she changed. Besides, She was young and kind of still is, but I know she learned from her mistakes.

When we finished eating breakfast, we left to the company.

"Good morning, Ms. Ferrari." Isabella greets me, before her eyes landing on Rebecca. "And you Ms.?"

"Rebecca." Becca smiles.

We enter my office and I motion for her to sit. I go and sit behind my desk. I kept on thinking of what role Rebecca could do in this company and I think I found the best. If I am not mistaken, Rebecca studied décor and design. This company is in need of redecorating and designing. She could be the one handling those stuff.

"Okay, so I have been thinking about your job and I found the best for you." I start, earning her attention. "My company is in serious need of change and redecorating, and that's where you come in. I heard that you studied this in university and I would like you to take the lead on this in my company." I finish. Her eyes sparkled in excitement and happiness.

"I would love that!" She excitedly claps.

"Great!" I say.

I pick up the phone, calling Isabella. I need Isabella to arrange a room close to mine for Rebecca to work.

I hear a knock, as I call for her to come in. Once she does, I say, "Isabella, I need you to arrange one of the rooms close to mine for Rebecca. She will be working here from now on." I say, earning a nod. She turns around to leave but I stop her,

"Oh, by the way, Rebecca is my sister."

* * *

Hey guys!!!! sorry for the last/short update, but I really want to take my time before Alessandro and Amalia meet again, BUT! it will be soon (maybe next chapter). I hope you liked this one and this story is on it's way to end. Few chapters are left.

What do you think will happen in the end?

Word count: 1481

# 23. "I Fucking Missed You"

ALESSANDRO

It has been almost two months since I last saw her. I am still in Florence close to Demetrio. He hasn't left, yet. He wants to make sure everything is okay and that all of us are safe. The thought of Amalia being by herself in Sicily, angers me. What is someone attacks her? She only has those useless guards around her and not me.

Why is she pushing me away? I know she feels guilty and is scared of what might happen to me and my daughter, but Lily and I are my responsibility. Whether she likes it or not, Lily's and my life are either way in danger. They know about us.

I couldn't stay away from her. After hearing her voice yesterday, I realized how stupid I was. I shouldn't have listened to her and I should have just went to her house and forced her to let me stay with her. Me being away doesn't do anything. The fact that I am still in Florence beside Demetrio says it all. We are all still in danger.

"Daddy!" Lily's voice echoes through the room. I stand up and walk towards her room, where she is calling from. I open the door and find her trying to tie her hair.

"What are you doing?" I ask, confusedly.

"Help me with my hair." I oblige without further questioning. I help her tie her hair and once we finished, she turns around and looks deeply into my eyes. "We are leaving," is all she said.

"Leaving, where?" I ask, furrowing my brows.

"To Sicily - to Amalia." She replies, getting her backpack from the bed. What is she doing?

"What do you mean "going to Sicily"?" I ask. Am I about to be controlled by an almost 5-year-old girl?

"Come on, daddy. We have to go to Amalia, I miss her and clearly, you too." She says, as a matter of fact.

Without much hesitation, I quickly run to my room and grab a small backpack and put the essential stuff. I take our passports and some money, and run to the living room. Lily is waiting for me impatiently.

I turn off all the lights and we leave the house. I make sure to send Demetrio a message telling him of what idea Lily came up with. I still can't believe that she was willing to literally maybe leave without me. I should thank her because without her, I wouldn't do this step. One thing I was afraid off is going to Amalia and she doesn't agree to speak with me. I couldn't handle it, especially after seeing her. But not that Lily's with me, I highly doubt Amalia will say no.

I buy two plane first class tickets from Florence to Sicily. The closest plane departing is in one hour, which is good. We go and sit in a restaurant in the airport and eat a little meal.

"I can't wait to see her, Daddy." Lily says, breaking my heart. I didn't know that she is too attached to Amalia. I knew she loved her a lot, but not like this. This makes me more determined and confident to go to Amalia and even if she disagrees to talk to me, I will make her. I will show her that we are safe - that no harm will comes to us, and that we are stronger together.

After 30 minutes, we were called to the gates. Lily and I walk into the gate, as we get scanned by a machine. We soon were allowed to enter the plane. Thank god, we don't have a lot of luggage. Just two small backpacks.

sitting on our seats, we buckle up and wait for departure.

* * *

The plane just landed and Lily and I make our way out of the airport. We find a taxi outside waiting for anyone to ask for him and we do. I walk towards him, making sure Lily's beside me. I ask if he's free and he says yes. We step into the car and I give him the address.

Suddenly, I feel nervous. So nervous. What will Amalia's reaction be? I know she won't be happy in the sense that she doesn't want us to be in danger, but I know she'll be happy to see us. I know she misses us because we do. A lot.

"Daddy, calm down." Lily's voice pulls me out of my thoughts. Sometimes, I really think Lily is too young for her brain. I mean...

"I am, sweetie." I try to act not nervous but she shakes her head.

"I should be the one nervous." She mutters.

"No, you absolutely shouldn't. Amalia could never say no or kick you out—" I say, "—but she could do with me." I mutter the last part, making sure Lily doesn't hear me.

The car suddenly stops and my heart raced till the sky. Do I regret coming? Of course, not. I could never. Amalia is the woman that I love and I will do anything to get her back.

I pay the man and step out of the car, making sure Lily leaves first. The last thing I want is him driving off with her still in the car and kidnapping her. Not judging or anything, but I don't trust anyone.

We stand in front of the big mansion that I worked in few months ago and a smile covers my lips. Finally!

"Daddy, come on." Lily nags, impatiently.

We walk towards the door and ring the bell. We don't hear any sound at first, when suddenly I heard Amalia's. "I'll get it!" She says.

After few seconds, the door flys open, revealing a very serious Amalia. Once her eyes landed on us, she is taken aback, almost like not believing herself.

"Nanny Amalia!" Lily shrieked, running towards Amy and hugging her. Amalia doesn't hug her at first, but her hands quickly wrapped around my daughter's body.

"Lily." Amalia breathes, heavily.

"I have missed you." Lily says, kissing Amalia on the cheek. Lucky girl.

After breaking the hug, Amalia's gaze lands on me and the reaction she gives me is not what I expected. She is standing there with a shy gaze, red cheeks.

"Alessandro." She almost stuttered, putting a piece of hair behind her ear.

She's shy.

"Come in." She says.

We walk in and the smell of the house reminded me of when I was working here. I remember the good and bad moments. I also remember the first time I came here and saw Amalia. She was too serious.

We walk to the living room to find her sister Rebecca sitting. I remember Rebecca from when she came and Amalia kick her out, while pulling her hair. That was a scene.

I am shocked to see her here since Amalia practically hates her.

"Hello." She greets with a smile and I greet her back.

"Who is she Nanny Amalia?" Lily asks.

"This is my sister, Rebecca—Rebecca, this is Lily, Alessandro's daughter." Amalia introduces.

"Hello, Lily." Rebecca kneels to Lily's level and shakes her hand.

"Lily, stay here with Rebecca, you dad and I are going to talk a little, okay?" Amalia says, earning a nod from Lily.

We grabs my arm and we walk outside to the backyard. Once she stops, she lets go of my arm and is about to say something when I cut her off.

"I fucking missed you." I say, crashing my lips onto hers with much force. She hesitates at first, but eventually kisses me back with passion. The kiss held everything, anger, love, and longing.

"Me too." She says, once we break the kiss. She is breathing heavily and so am I.

"You shouldn't have come here, Alessandro." Her voice cracks.

"I will not leave you, Amalia. I can't." I reply. "I have missed you so much and my life has been so bad that I couldn't sleep. I want you, hell, I need you." I add.

"What if something happens?—" A tears escapes, landing on her cheek. "What if they kidnap Lily again?"

"No one is kidnapping anyone. They are in jail—besides, we work together. We solve this together." I say, caressing her cheeks.

"I love you." She blurts out, making me the happiest man in the world.

I lean in until my lips graze her ear and say, "Ti amo e ti adoro, crazzo," making her smile brightly.

"You have been learning." She grins.

"Of course, I have."

* * *

I hope you enjoyed this chapter!!!!!

I will try to daily update until the story finishes! Probably four or five chapters more

Word count: 1444

# 24. Rebecca

AMALIA

It has been two days since Alessandro and Lily arrived and I still cannot believe my eyes. I am so happy they came even when I tried so hard to push them away. Pushing them away made me realize that I couldn't live without them.

I wake up the next day with Gus wrapped around my body. I miss him so much and I cannot help but feel that I am not spending time with him like before. I lean in and give him a quick kiss before getting out of bed to the bathroom. Alessandro didn't stay with me because I told him he should sleep with his daughter. To be honest, I didn't trust anyone with Lily other than him and me. I didn't want to leave her to sleep alone too.

I freshen up, taking a quick shower and brushing my teeth. I wrap the soft pink towel around my body and leave to my walk-in closet. I look around my clothes and I couldn't help but feel that I need to go shopping. I haven't done that in a long time. I decide to wear a simple mid-thigh black dress, pairing it with black heels. I quickly dry my hair with the hair-dryer and apply a little but of makeup like I do everyday.

I look at the mirror and once I am satisfied with myself, I leave the room. I was so excited to see Alessandro that I didn't see him coming our of his room and bumping into him like the clumsy person I am.

"Good morning." I nervously say, earning a chuckle. He suddenly cages me, making my back hit the wall, and leans in.

"I like when you get all nervous around me--it's sexy." He says, huskily. His morning voice is making me feel things...so many things. Could he get any sexier?

"Alessandro--" I scold, "What if Lily comes out and sees us." I whisper.

He laughs, as if he knows I am only saying this because I am nervous; which is true. I know that Lily won't say anything and probably would be so happy.

He leans in without hesitation and kisses my neck, seductively, making my moan loudly. Fuck!

He keeps sucking and kissing my neck, as if his life depended on it. I wrap my arms around his neck, as one of them creeps to his hair. I couldn't control my moans, as he hits the right spot in my neck. I feel my body getting hot and I wanted nothing other than him right now. I need him.

Just as he is about to smash his lips onto mine, Lily's voice echoes in the hallway.

"Daddy? Amy?" She says, hesitantly.

I quickly push him off and plaster a smile on my face. "Hello, sweetie." I say, walking towards her and hugging her.

"What were you two doing?" She asks, furrowing her brows.

I am about to answer, when Alessandro beats me to it, "We were making love, baby." He smirks, knowing how red my face is going to be after he says that. I find it hard to calm myself down, but eventually do when I hear what Lily says next.

"Finally!" She huffs, hiding a smile. She amazes me every time. I fucking love her.

"Umm, let's go down for breakfast." I say, smiling.

She puts her hand in mine; which I find it very cute and calming, and walk downstairs, leaving Alessandro behind. We soon hear him grunt, making us laugh silently.

"Good morning, Ms. Ferrari." Ashelia greets, handing my the tea, but I told her to put it on the breakfast table. Ever since Annie died, Ashelia has been handing me my tea every morning. I didn't want her to do that, but she insisted. I never argued with her and agreed.

We walk to the table and sit down. Soon after, Rebecca enters and sits. "Good morning." She says with a smile.

"Good morning." I reply, sipping my tea.

I turn to Alessandro and say, "Unfortunately for today, I have to leave to the office, but after that, I'll take few days off." I say.

"Can we come with you?" Lily asks, pouting. It made my heart clench and I couldn't tell her no. Just as Alessandro is about to answer her, I say, "Of course, both of you can come."

After we finish breakfast, all of us walk out towards the car. I made sure to dress Lily up, since Alessandro was doing a terrible job. God...I have to teach him or otherwise, he'd dress up Lily in her Pjs and takes her out. I mean...I wonder what he would do when we have...

Shit....

We arrive at the company, making our way inside. As we get inside, everyone looks our way, surprised that I came with other people, especially with a young girl. As much as my attitude changed towards everyone at home, it didn't with my employees. I am still the scary Amalia everyone avoids; that's besides Isabella.

We step into the elevator, pressing my floor.

"I like this place." Lily says with her cute voice.

"I am glad you do." I smile, giving her a kiss. If only she knows that everything is for her.

The elevator dinged, indicating that we arrived to my floor. We step out and I greet Isabella once my eyes lands on her. "Good morning, Isabella. Come to my office please." I say.

"Sandro, could you please wait in Rebecca's room with Lily?" I say, earning a confused look. He nods and they walk away towards Rebecca's room.

Isabella and I walk to my office and once I close the door, she immediately says, "Ms. Ferrari, the contract was stolen."

I look at her with the a calm expression. She furrows her eyebrows, taken aback from my reaction.

"You knew?—I swear I didn't stea-"

"Isabella, relax, I know you didn't." I quickly say, before she cries. One thing I discovered is that Isabella tears up really fast.

"What do you mean?" She asks, clearly confused.

"I know you didn't steal it because I trust you Isabella." I say, proudly, earning a smile.

"Then who did it?" She asks, thinking too hard.

"There are only three people in this floor—you, me, and Rebecca." As soon as I say this, her eyes widen.

"Are you saying..."

I nod.

"Why do you think I gave her a job here?" I ask, amused.

"Because she's your sister?" She replies, as I roll my eyes.

"Of course, not. After what she did in the past; which you don't know of, I would let her back in my life without testing her in some way, wouldn't I?" I explain.

"But why would she do that?"

"I don't know, but I will find out—besides, she's a bitch and will always be a bitch."

A laugh escapes her lips, but quickly shuts herself up once I look her way. She keeps looking at me, trying to see if I am mad when I break out laughing. She joins me later on.

* * *

ALESSANDRO

"Daddy, where is Amy?" Lily asks, pouting.

"She has a little bit of work. She will come in few minutes, okay?" I reply, earning a nod.

I still don't understand why Amalia didn't want me and Lily to join her, didn't she trust us? Of course, not. She does trust us, but I am sure there is something going on. I glance at Rebecca, who's sitting nervously in her chair, not uttering a word. I grow suspicious. If one thing Amalia and I shared in common is that we understood each other and we are extremely paranoid...in a good kind of way.

"Daddy, bathroom, please." Lily pulls me out of my thoughts. I take her hand in mine and we leave Rebecca's office. I look around until I find the bathroom sign. We walk to the bathroom and go in.

Lily walks to the stall and sits to do her business. I thank god that she is smart enough to do it her own.

"Daddy." Lily calls.

"Yes, baby?"

"I want to say something." She starts. "I want Amalia to be my new mother, please."

My eyes widen at her request. Is she really requesting a new mother like she is requesting me to buy her a new toy? I want to laugh so bad.

"Umm..." I scratch the back of my neck.

"Don't say no. I want her to be my mother. She loves me and I love her." She commands, making me chuckle.

"Well, I love her and she loves me too, a lot." I smirk, remembering what happened this morning.

"Then, okay?"

"Okay, baby."

We walk back to Rebecca's office to see Amalia and Isabella standing there. Rebecca is a crying mess. She is begging Amalia for something that I didn't understand. I quickly take Lily's hand and take her to Amalia's office.

"Stay here, baby, okay?" She nods and I close the door.

"What's happening?" I ask as soon as I reach the office. No one answers.

"Did you really think I wouldn't know?" Amalia questions her sister. "Did you think that I have a soft soot for you? Because I don't." Amalia chuckles. For a second, all I could see is the old Amalia and as much as I love the new Amalia, I am fucking obsessed with the old.

I look at her with amusement.

"Do you know what will happen, sister?" She asks. She has a smirk on her face, an evil one. "I will hand you into the police."

"You don't have a proof of anything!" Rebecca screams, wiping her tears.

"And who said I couldn't create new evidence?" Amalia smirks, as Rebecca's face covered in fear.

"Y-you can't do that."

"Oh, darling. You will don't know me well." Amalia says.

* * *

"I can't believe you did that." I say once Amalia and I are alone. Lily is with Isabella playing somewhere.

"Don't tell me I am heart-less." She snaps, angrily. I chuckle, earning a glare. I walk towards her and cage her just like I did in the morning. I know she hates it because she feels helpless, but I know secretly she loves being in my arms.

"I am not in the mood." She mutters.

I caress her cheek, as I kiss her other one. "I am absolutely obsessed with you, Amalia." Her name rolls out of my tongue.

"Ha?" She asks, still in a haze.

"I love the mean, manipulative, Amalia. I fucking love all of you..." I say, huskily, as I continue my kisses onto her neck.

"Really?" She asks, breathless.

"Really." I grin.

"Then, let's go home." She smirks and I immediately knew what she has in mind.

* * *

Hey guys! Another chapter

I hope you like it.

Word count: 1815

# 25. Sad but Happy

AMALIA

Have you ever been sad but happy? Well, I have. I am so sad that I don't have family left. That my sister had betrayed me once again for reasons I don't know of. Was she even working with Franco and Gino? Who knows. Did she want me dead like the others? Who knows. But what I know, is that she will serve for the rest of her life in jail for crimes she didn't even commit expect for fraud and stealing. I made sure to put her in jail for the rest of her life. On the other hand, I am very happy. Happy that I have a new family here with me. Alessandro, Lily, and Isabella, are my new family. Yes, Isabella...shocking, right? At least, she hasn't betrayed me, yet.

"Yesterday is the best night of my life." Alessandro murmurs, while wrapping his arms around my naked figure. Being in bed with him is all I ask for for the rest of my life.

"Me too." I whisper back, hugging him tightly.

"You know, it just occurred to me that I have never met your mother." I say, looking at him. A smirk appears on his beautiful lips, making me confused.

"What?" I grin.

"Are you that eager to meet her?" His smirk doesn't for once leave his face.

"Y-yeah...I guess. Why? does she hate me?" I frown, trying to calm my racing heart.

"What? of course, not." He quickly replies. "What I mean is that is the reason for your eagerness is to you know...be closer to me...like you know...wife." I jerk back, feeling flushed. My cheeks burn with embarrassment, as I couldn't look at his eyes.

"W-umm...that's no-" I chuckle, nervously.

"Relax, baby." He laughs, pulling me closer to him. The contact of my body with his make my insides burn with need. I have never felt like this before. This feeling is too foreign. Yes, I have had a boyfriend before...unfortunately...but it wasn't like this. This is too much and the fact that I am getting attached and he is too, is too scary. But I am too selfish to walk away. I want him all for me. Imagine me leaving him for other women, who will waste no time into getting him.

Fuck...even just thinking about it, angers me.

"You know, I am really surprised Gus let me sleep here today." He says, changing the subject.

"I told you he'll warm up." I laugh, placing my head in the crook of his neck.

All of a sudden, the door flies open revealing Lily. "Daddy, weren't you sleeping with me?" Her cute morning voice echoes through the room.

"I was, baby. But I woke up and came here." He replies.

"Why?" She demands, making me chuckle.

"You remember what you told me in the bathroom few days ago?" He asks, smirking like an idiot. What the fuck did she tell him? I want to know.

"Yes." She replies.

"Yeah, I am working on that." He sends her a wink, making her giggle. she runs towards us and jumps on the bed. I quickly hide my naked body, making sure she doesn't see me naked.

"Amy, I miss you. Sleep with us tonight." Lily says, making me smile brightly.

"I miss you too, baby - How about you two sleep here tonight?" I say, cupping her cheeks, earning a nod.

"Really?" Alessandro asks, shocked from my question.

"Yes, why not." I send him a wink, earning a giggle back from Lily.

* * *

The door bell rings, grabbing our attention. Lily yells happily, as she ran towards the door, as she couldn't keep her excitement at bay. She was so excited to see Demetrio and Leila again. The past couple of months, Alessandro told me that they stayed in Florence for a couple of months and there, Lily got so attached to Demetrio and Leila. I was happy to hear that.

I stand up from my seat and walk towards the door to great the Gonzalez's. They are visiting us today to eat dinner and talk about some important matters.

"Welcome!" I greet Leila and Demetrio, giving him a hug.

"Good evening!" Demetrio greets.

"I have finally seen you two together again." Leila says, pointing at Alessandro and I, making me blush.

They follow us to the dining room, while Lily shares few stories of when they first arrived here. I take a seat beside Alessandro, leaving Demetrio to sit at the head of the table. Even though, this is my house, I have a huge respect for older people and Demetrio being like a father to me, he has to sit there.

"Thanks, dear." He thanks me. I nod.

We start eating the food Ezekiel made, which by the way, is delicious. I still cannot believe that Ezekiel endured working for me. I mean...I was pretty hard on him at first. I remember this one time when I heard him telling Annie that he wants to quit, but she convinced him not to because she knew I loved his food.

Ugh...Annie.

If only you knew that I was right about Rebecca all that time. I am really glad that Annie is no longer here because I couldn't take her disappointed face when she learns that Rebecca is worse than before.

"Amy..." Lily's voice pulls me out of my thoughts.

"Yes, sweetie?" I reply, as everyone's attention is on us now.

"Can I call you, mommy?"

I sit, frozen to my seat, as the whole room becomes silent. Lily kept looking at me, waiting for me to say something. Was I happy that she wanted to call me mommy? Absolutely. Was I nervous of Alessandro's reaction? Definitely.

I clear my throat and glance at Alessandro to ask for approval, when I find him smiling like an idiot. I quickly glance at Lily and say, "do you really want to?" I ask softly. She nods.

"Then, you can call me, mommy." I smile, as she cheered and stands up and runs towards me for a hug. I hug her back with much excitement as hers.

"What have you done with my daughter." Alessandro teases.

"The real question is, what has she done with both of you." Demetrio says, making us all laugh.

* * *

After dinner, Leila stayed with Lily in the living room, while Alessandro, Demetrio and I talked about certain matter in my office.

"Are you sure we are safe?" Alessandro asks.

"I am—" Demetrio replies and continues, "—I have kidnapped everyone who is a member of the circle and investigated them. No one is involved from them—I also talked to few small mafias around Sicily and made sure no one touches any of you. You also have their protection and mine."

I sign in relief.

"Thank you, Demetrio. So much. I don't know what would I have done without you." I say, hugging him. He means the world to me and without him, I wouldn't have gotten rid of my past.

"Your welcome, mi hija." He replies, hugging me back.

"Can I have a hug too?" Alessandro jokes, making me chuckle at his playfulness.

"You get to get more than that." I wink at him.

"Okay, both of you are acting like Mia and River, and it is annoying." Demetrio cringes, making us laugh. He leaves the office back to his wife.

"Now that we are alone..." Alessandro murmurs, grabbing me by my waist, holding me tightly.

"Don't even think about it." I say, firmly.

"Why?" He pouts.

"I am playing hard to get." I smirk, pushing him back and leave the office.

I walk back to the living room and I could hear footsteps behind me. I see Lily playing with Leila and I smile at the scene. I hope one day I become like Leila. She had endured so many things, yet she is still standing up on her feet and having a smile on her face. She is so lucky to have Demetrio and I am so lucky to have Alessandro. Well...they are also lucky to have us.

"Mommy!" Lily squeals once she sees me. She stands up from the floor and runs towards me, hugging my legs. My heart flutters at what she said. She called me mommy and it is taking everything in me not to cry in happy tears right now.

"Baby." I kneel to her level and give her a kiss on the cheek. She giggles and glances at her father before running and hugging him. She whispers something in his ear, making his cheeks turn red.

I am so curious now and I want to know. Why do they keep whispering? God...

"Amalia, honey. We have to leave now, but I'll see you soon for sure." Leila says.

"Thank you for coming and for everything." I say, hugging them both.

"See you and take care." Demetrio says and they leave.

Once they leave, I close the door behind them and turn around and walk to the living room. I see Alessandro and Lily playing on the floor with Lily's barbies.

I walk towards them and sit on the floor beside Lily. Alessandro sends me a smile before looking back at the dolls.

"Amy, I am baby, you are mommy, and he is daddy, okay?" She commands, handing the dolls to each one of us.

I nod shyly and we start playing together.

* * *

Hey guys! I hope you like this chapter!!! Two more chapters before the story ends. I really hoped to write more, but unfortunately, I feel the story is good here.

I hope you liked it

Word count: 1615

* * *

# 26. Happily

ALESSANDRO

I have done this before, but this time is different. Indeed, I was so nervous to propose to Amanda, but Amalia is a whole different story. I am shaking and the fact that tonight I will ask for her hand is just nerve racking. Maybe because of the fact that she can do better than me. She can find a better person, or the fact that she can live without me in some way. She doesn't need me, is what I mean to say.

My whole life, I have never thought that I would meet the perfect woman. I didn't even think of Amanda as an amazing, wonderful, loving, or caring woman. In fact, of it wasn't for Lily, I might have filed a divorce a long time ago. It was only for Lily that I stayed with Amanda a little while till I couldn't anymore. And now meeting Amalia, changed my perspective of everything. Gosh...she is just something else.

The first time I met Amalia here, she captivated my heart. From the first glance, I suddenly knew she was the one. Her mean, dominating, power lover personality, just allured me towards her like a magnet. There was and still is something in her that makes me want her forever. That makes me want to know her even more than she knows herself. There is something that makes me want to protect her at all times despite the money she has to get as many bodyguards as she wants. But she chose me. When she told me that we had met before and how she had a little crush on me, I lost it. I couldn't believe that I didn't notice her, when again, I was with Amanda.

I look to my right to see Lily sleeping. I want so badly to sneak to Amalia's room, but decided against it. So, I decided to text her.

Me: hey, baby. Are you asleep?"

I send the message and wait for her to reply. I really hope she isn't sleeping. I miss her like hell. As if on cue, my phone vibrates.

Lia: fuck, I was thinking about you.

Her text made me smile. I wonder what was she thinking about me.

Me: what were you thinking about me?

Lia: Of course, I am not saying that. Playing hard to get, remember?

I chuckle.

Me: so, you are telling me that you don't want me to come to your room right now?

I send the message and wait for her reply. I am one hundred percent sure she wouldn't say no because she wants me so bad as much as I want her. She doesn't reply for a while, clearly contemplating what to say. Suddenly, my phone vibrates.

Lia: no.

I didn't think she would actually say no...I mean?

I am about to reply, when suddenly, the door opens and there she is, standing with only her night gown, looking sexy as hell. She tiptoes inside the room towards the bed and slides under the cover beside me and Lily. The thing is, we were supposed to sleep with Amalia tonight, but Lily was playing in this room on the bed and fell asleep. So, I really didn't think of taking her to the next room when she is already sleeping comfortable.

"I knew you couldn't stay away from me for long." I whisper in her ear, making her body shudder in pleasure.

"Shut-up." She whispers back, while trailing kisses down my neck, making it hard for me to bite my moans.

I wrap my arm around her tiny waist, pulling her closer to my chest. Our chests make contact and the only thing that I want to do right now is to remove that piece of night gown. Trust me, that's not the only thing that I think about when it comes to Amalia. I always think about her beautiful smart mind and witty personality. She is everything I have ever dreamt of.

"Lia..." I try to bite my moan, but couldn't anymore. I quickly glance at my daughter to make sure she's asleep. "Let's go to your room." I say and take her hand.

We quickly make our way to her room and once we're in, I close the door and push her against the wall, kissing her neck, hungrily. Fuck...

She pulls my face to her level and smashes her lips onto mine. One thing I love about Amalia is that she knows what's she doing and she likes to dominate.

We end up on the bed, on top of each other, kissing hungrily like teenage kids.

"Alessandro..." She calls, breathlessly.

"Yes?"

"I need you."

* * *

We are currently on our way to my mother's house. Amalia is so nervous because it is her first time meeting my mother. To be honest, I have told my mother about Amalia before and she is so excited to meet her. She was so happy when I told her that I met the love of my life. She was a little bit scared, especially after Amanda, but I assured her that Amalia is nothing like Amanda.

"Calm down, baby." I soothe, drawing circle in the palm of her hand.

"I am so nervous, I don't even know why - What if she doesn't like me? What if she wants me out of your life?" She fires questions, making me laugh, as she scowls.

"Don't laugh at me." She growls, hitting me on the arm.

I fucking love her playful side.

"You're so cute when you're angry." I mumble, kissing her on the cheek.

After the plane landed in Florence, we take a taxi to my mother's house. Lily is sleeping and I hold her in my arms as we step into the taxi cab.

"Has she told you anything about me?" Lia suddenly asks.

I turn her way and smile, "She is so excited to meet you, don't worry, baby."

After an hour, we arrive at my mother's house. She lives in a two-story house all by herself. I told her to come and live in Sicily, but she declined, claiming that Florence is safer, which is unfortunately true. She also has all her friends here in Florence.

"Calm down." I say, as I wake up Lily with my hand.

"I think I am gonna faint." She breathes, heavily. I want to laugh so badly, but I control myself.

Lily wakes up and I pay the taxi driver. We step out of the car and walk towards the door. Before we could even knock, the door flies open, revealing a very happy and excited mother. She looks between us three, as her gaze lands on Amalia. A grin appears on her lips, as she took Amalia in for a hug. Amalia is shook for sure... She didn't even expect this.

"Welcome, darling!" My mother beams. She then looks at Lily and hugs her.

"Aren't you going to greet me, mother?" I say, offended.

"I'll think about it." She replies, making us all laugh, including Lia.

She gives me a hug and invites us in. I miss her home. It feels homey and the smell of rosewood is everywhere. My lovely mother had moved to Florence when I divorced Amanda. Since I am Italian, we had already had this house ready for any occasion.

"You are even more beautiful than what Alessandro told me." My mother says to Amalia, making her blush.

"Thanks, ma'am." Lia replies, making my mother frown.

"Call me Emily, please." She smiles, earning a nod.

"Is Cassie here?" I ask, looking for my sister.

"She is in England for a vacation. She's coming next week."

"I made dinner for all of you, please follow me."

We follow my mother to the dining room and sit. My mother sits at the head of the table, I on her left, Amalia on her right, and Lily beside me.

"It is so good to have you all here." My mother tears up.

"Don't make me cry, mother." I try to joke, succeeding as she smiles.

"I would like to thank you Amalia for taking care of my boy."

"Oh, it's nothing. In fact, he took care of me. Without him, I wouldn't be here." Amalia replies, shyly.

After we finish dinner, I put sleepy Lily on her bed, closing the door behind me. Thank god, Amalia and I are sharing a room. I cannot wait to have her in my arms.

"I want to show you something." I tell her.

"What?"

"Follow me."

I take her hand and walk towards the back of the house. My father had built a smile tree house that I used to play in as a kid. It is still here because my mother couldn't get rid of it and neither could I.

"Where are we going?" She asks, impatiently.

"You'll see."

Soon, we reach the tree house and I step in with Amalia behind me.

"This is so beautiful." She mumbles, as she looks around. Her eyes sparkle as they make their way to me.

I sit on the ground and motion for her to do so. I am so nervous of what I am about to say and my heart races. What if she says no? I try to muster the courage and look her in the eye.

"Lia."

"Yes?"

"Remember when you praised me for getting better at Italian?" I ask, nervously.

"Yes."

"I didn't learn it just for fun, I learned it to ask you something."

"Alessandro, just spit it out." She snaps.

"Mo vuoi sposare, Amalia Ferrari?"

* * *

GUYS! I hope you like this chapter! One more to go!!!!

DISCLAIMER: I just want to mention that even thought Alessandro is Italian, he doesn't know the full language. His father died when he was young, so he didn't learn the whole language.

Also, I am not sure if I mentioned when his father died or not, but just pretend that <3

Word count: 1647

# 27. Married | Ending |

Recap

"Remember when you praised me for getting better at Italian?" I ask, nervously.

"Yes."

"I didn't learn it just for fun, I learned it to ask you something."

"Alessandro, just spit it out." She snaps.

"Mo vuoi sposare, Amalia Ferrari?"

* * *

AMALIA

"Sei serio?!" I ask, my eyes are about to leave the socket. (Are you serious?)

He nervously plays with his hands and says, "of course—only if you want to." The ring box is still hanging in his hand.

I look at him in disbelief. Annie had always told me to marry and have kids and I had always told her that it's impossible. That no one would love the Amalia Ferrari. That no one could keep up with me and my personality. But here he is, the love of my life, proposing to me in his childhood tree house. In Italian.

"Amalia?" His voice echoes, desperation could be heard. He is scared and I don't blame him because I don't say anything for a while. "I am s-sorry...I-" he starts, putting the box away.

I cut him off and smash my lips onto his. He is taken aback and doesn't kiss me back, but once he's aware, his lips move and deepens the kiss. Our mouths dance together, unable to break the kiss.

Soon, we break the kiss to catch breath. "Amalia?" He murmurs, cupping my cheeks.

"Yes." My voice says, shocking me. He doesn't get it thinking that I said yes to him calling me, where I was saying yes to his question. He looks at me for a while, unsure of what to say.

"Yes, Alessandro. Yes, I would love to marry you." As soon as the words leave my mouth, a smile stretches on his lips, making my heart flutter. He leans in and hugs me tightly, not wanting to break the hug at all. We stay like this for few minutes, until he leans back and looks intently at me. Then then takes out a box from his pocket again and it reveals a ring. He takes it out of the box and put it on my ring finger. A beautiful small diamond. He obviously knew that I don't like a big one.

"I fucking love you, Amalia Ferrari." He whispers.

"Ti voglio bene, Alessandro Esposito." I whisper back, giving him another kiss. (I fucking love you back)

* * *

We walk back inside, seeing Lily long asleep on the couch. Emily is beside her, as she scrolls down on her phone. "Oh, there you are." She whispers, once she sees us.

"What took you so long?" She asks.

I raise my hand and show her the finger. Her eyes widen is delight, as she looks at the finger with awe. It looks like she couldn't believe that her son is finally marrying a good woman; not trying to brag or anything.

"Finally!" She yells, startling Lily, who wakes up all confused.

"What's happening?" Lily asks in her night voice. I do the same thing I did with Emily and she looks even more confused.

"Did you say you wanted Amalia to me your mother?Alessandro asks, shocking the hell out of me. I didn't know that Lily wanted Alessandro to marry me, even when she even calls me mommy.

"Yes." She replies, nodding.

"We are getting married." He announces and her face lit up.

"You finally mommy mommy?" She asks, her mouth wide open. I nod.

She runs my way, hugging my legs tightly. She seems so happy. "So we are going to live together?" She grins. I nod again.

She squeals and hugs her father. "Thanks, papa." She says in Italian, which melts my heart.

"Now, go to sleep. We have to sleep too." Sandro says.

We walk to our room after tucking Lily in. The room is super cozy, making me feel warm. Emily didn't let us go to a hotel, so we are staying here. I mean, it is the only logical thing to do.

I open my small suitcase and take out a night gown. A black lace night gown. I know Alessandro will eye-rape me because he loves this night gown. He always compliments me whenever he sees me wearing it.

I walk back into the room after washing my face, to see him lying on the bed, shirtless. He looks up at me once I walk in and he jerks upfront in a sitting position, as if he couldn't see what he's seeing.

"Holy shit." He mumbles, looking at me, as if I am a hamburger.

I walk towards the other side of the bed and plump down. I slid under the covers and immediately a hand touches my body, wrapping around my waist, and pulling me firmly. I am now glued to Alessandro's body tightly. I try to move but he keeps his strong hold. "Dare to move again and I swear I'll take you right here right now." He growls, as he leans in, pressing his forehead on mine. I inhale deeply because I couldn't calm my racing heart. It was too much. He closes his eyes and I do the same thing. All of a sudden, out lips meet as if our faces were magnets, pulling each other in the same direction.

We fight for dominance, but I end up winning, of course. We keep kissing, this kiss becoming urgent, passionate, and rough. We break away to breathe a little and press our foreheads again together.

"Fuck, I am falling in love with you more every second." He whispers, nuzzling my nose with his.

"Alessandro." I call.

"Mhmm." He hums, still in a haze.

"I need you."

* * *

Two month later

Pain.

The worst thing that could happen to a person is losing their loved ones.

I look into the screen as the woman kept crying for her dead husband. I couldn't imagine this happening to me. I'd die.

I am a crying mess.

"Baby, it's only a movie, don't cry." Alessandro whispers, kissing my beck softly. I keep crying.

"He's dead." I cry even more.

"Your hormones are all over the place, baby, and I like it." He chuckles, making me frown.

"You're happy that I am crying?" I ask, wiping the smile of his face. He frowns and immediately sits up to explain.

"I don't mean that, baby, it's just it's cute to see you crying over this movie." He explains, nervously, making me smile evilly. I quickly hide the smile and frown again.

"You can't say that!" I fake cry now. I am so moody right now. You could blame it all on that I am pregnant.

Yes, pregnant. Just discovered two weeks ago. It was pretty fast and I guess I should consider myself lucky. I am.

"I am sorry, baby. Please, forgive me." He says, worriedly. He looks so cute and so innocent.

I lean in and give him a peck. "I was just kidding, baby."

This time, he frowns and playfully slaps my hand. He then leans in and kisses me on the cheek, which later went to my next, etc.

"You're naughty, you know that, right?" He whispers, making me giggle.

Suddenly, a baby voice echoes through the living room. I look up and see my baby. Lily.

"Mommy! Daddy!" She calls, running towards us, giving us a big group hug.

Well, that's our life now. Happily Married.

Love,

Amalia.

* * *

Heyooo! This is the last chapter of this story guys! I thank each and everyone of you who stayed with me throughout it all! It really means a lot and thanks for the love! I appreciate it.

I know this chapter is not too good for an ending, but I suck at endings anyway.

I would like to ask you a question:

Would you like a story for Lily?

Thanks,

Love you

* * *

CPSIA information can be obtained
at www.ICGtesting.com
Printed in the USA
LVHW030318160223
739598LV00019B/1543

9 781918 112283